Praise for *A*

"*Along the Path of Torment* is a
with moments of surprising t........ Morrison dials up the noir
and writes his characters with careful attention to what haunts them.
Like a Bret Easton Ellis novel that refuses to fetishize the toxic
glamor of LA and its shadow worlds, *Along the Path of Torment* is
memorable and intriguing."
—Lindsay Lerman, Author of *I'm From Nowhere*

"Chandler Morrison's most disturbing book yet (and that's saying
something!), packed with loathsome characters, cancerous truths,
and all-too-plausible Hollywood sleaze."
—Christine Morgan, Author of *Lakehouse Infernal*

"*Along the Path of Torment* is a masterful odyssey of Hollywood deca-
dence and depravity, an unflinching and often morbidly hilarious
plunge into the void as Chandler Morrison explores the harsh truths
of power in an increasingly soulless and decaying world."
—Ryan Harding, Author of *Genital Grinder*

Praise for *Dead Inside*

"Chandler Morrison is one of the most visceral and uncompromis-
ing writers of his generation, and *Dead Inside* is a nightmarish, unfor-
gettable work of fiction."
—Donald Ray Pollock, Author of *The Devil All the Time*

"Not since Peter Sotos' *Special* has a book lifted my brows like this.
This is Advanced Graduate Level Necrophilia, where mankind's
worst taboo is utilized as a vehicle for sociopolitical commentary,
not to mention a slap-in-the-face dose of outright subversion to remind the reader that the road to happiness doesn't end with IMAX
flicks, Facebook, and Red Lobster. Outrage, rampant political incor-
rectness, and misanthropy-as-life-direction are the moving parts by
which this engine runs. The easily offended be forewarned!"
—Edward Lee, Author of *The Bighead* and *The Pig*

"The writing style and story movement kept me coming back until the surprise ending . . . A most unusual and entertaining read."
—Judith O'Dea, Actress (*Night of the Living Dead*)

Praise for *Until the Sun*

"Full of pain, beauty, and some of the best prose I've read all year . . . If this is the new bar, the rest of us need to work a lot harder."
—Lucas Mangum, Author of *Saint Sadist* and *Gods of the Dark Web*

"A thoroughly riveting, thrilling, dark, twisted adventure of backstories, secrets, and all-around can't-put-it-down brilliance. Skillfully interwoven, character-rich, utterly believable."
—*The Horror Fiction Review*

"Colder than a mink glove and cooler than being cool. This book is ICE COLD."
—EconoClash Review

ALONG THE PATH OF TORMENT

OF

TORMENT

CHANDLER MORRISON

ATLATL

Atlatl Press
POB 521
Dayton, Ohio 45401
atlatlpress.com
info@atlatlpress.com

Along the Path of Torment
ISBN-13: 978-1-941918-69-2

For my LA mom, Kelley Harron

Also by Chandler Morrison

Dead Inside

Until the Sun

Hate to Feel

Just to See Hell

ALONG THE PATH OF TORMENT

"The only way to a woman's heart is along the path of torment."

— Marquis de Sade

ONE
THE POWER OF A NAME

LOS ANGELES is the only place I've been that feels truly alive. Like there's something shifting beneath the surface. Hungry, sinister. A black mass, chanting and groaning between the staccato blaring of car horns. It knows me. It wants me. It wants all of me.

It is an ugly thing, this city. It is everything I hate.

It is the only place I belong.

• • •

Standing outside the casting offices in the light rain, smoking a cigarette as discarded bits of trash swirl around me in the wind, I watch the slow chug of traffic on Wilshire. BMWs, Mercedes, Bentleys, Maseratis. Molten onyx, cherry scarlet, flaming canary. Even the way the rainwater slithers down the tinted windshields in silver rivulets is majestic.

I hate them all.

I hate them because they do not belong to me.

They should.

My phone vibrates, and I glance at it. A text from my uncle, commanding, *LET'S GO.* I've been gone all of five minutes.

My final drag from the cigarette is a beleaguered sigh.

• • •

"Filthy habit," Arthur says when I reenter the gray room on the fifteenth floor. "I can smell you all the way over here." He scowls at me. Tony, seated next to him at the long black table, nods his head in agreement.

I don't tell them it's a small room. I don't tell them I'm not standing that far away from them. I don't tell them to get fucked.

Arthur turns his attention to his laptop and clicks on something. "The next one is . . . Beatrice Rider." He grimaces at his screen. "Jesus, what a terrible name, yeah? Rider isn't bad, but *Beatrice*?" He sucks his teeth and shakes his head. "Whatever, bring her in."

• • •

Every time I open the door into the hallway waiting area, I want to kill myself. This is where capitalism has taken us. A long line of teenage girls waiting for rejection, their anxious faces dolled up and their blonde hair blown out. The try-hard mothers are no better; most of them are too old to be tanning like they do, and seriously, if you can't afford liposuction, don't wear fucking miniskirts.

"Beatrice Rider?" I say to the group. My voice, polite and inquisitive, is like a rotary saw grinding against metal. This is beneath me. This is not where I'm supposed to be.

The girl who stands up is largely indistinguishable from the rest, but an odd thing happens when her eyes find mine. There's something cold there, in her gaze. A shrewd intelligence beyond her years. I feel like she's trying to communicate something, to convey a message too monstrous for words. Everything slows down, goes quiet, and I'm on the verge of understanding when the spell is broken because the girl's mother—younger and prettier than the other mothers, but still not exceedingly fuckable—seizes her daughter's arm and whispers something into her ear. The girl makes a face, and when she turns back to me, she's the same as any other wannabe child actress—hopeful, naïve, with a vapid emptiness behind her eyes.

If my disappointment had a name, it would be Shame.

• • •

"My name is Arthur Seward," my uncle says, grinning at Beatrice. His tanned, Botoxed face strains with the effort, making him look like a leering skeleton. "I'm producing this commercial." He gestures at Tony and says, less enthusiastically, "This is the director, Tony Alonso." He pauses, leaning back in his chair and clicking his ballpoint pen. "I don't always bother with introductions—"

This is true. He doesn't, so I immediately know he likes her.

"—but I'm bothering with *you* for a specific reason." He runs his hand through his white hair. "Do you know what that reason is?"

"No, sir, I don't know," Beatrice says in her best jailbait voice. I resist the urge to roll my eyes and instead look out the floor-to-ceiling window at the tiny cars below. It's harder to hate them all the way up here because I can't really see them. Harder, but not impossible.

"It's because we have *good* names. *My* name, in particular, is *especially* good. It says something. Something about *me*. About who I *am*. It's . . . it's an *elite* name, yeah? It speaks to my *power*."

I've always hated our family's name. It makes me think of sewage. If it wasn't for what the name means in the industry, I'd have changed it a long time ago.

Also, Arthur sounds . . . old.

But I'm not here for my opinions.

"Do you know what *your* name says about you, *Beatrice*?"

"No, sir, I don't know." There's less confidence in the attempted lightness of the girl's voice this time, and I can't decide how it makes me feel.

"At best, it says nothing," Arthur says flatly, his mouth a thin, hard line. "At *worst*, it says you're a frigid, stuck-up cunt. Are you a frigid, stuck-up cunt, *Beatrice*?"

"No, sir, I am not," says Beatrice. I turn away from the window and look at her, and she intercepts my glance. It's not the same as whatever had happened in the hallway, but it's similar. A spark. A forbidden, unspeakable truth beyond my comprehension. Like she sees me, sees *into* me. I look back out the window.

"You should change it then, yeah?" says Arthur, his tone less severe. "All the best performers have stage names. Something like . . . something like *Dolly*. Yeah, that's good, isn't it, Tony?" Tony nods dutifully. "Dolly Rider. A name like that, the possibilities are endless, utterly *endless*. Say the acting gig doesn't work out, you hit the pole." He chuckles and holds up his hand. "The *chrome* pole, of course—not its, ah, fleshy counterpart. Save that for a last resort, yeah? Still, if you gotta go that route, you certainly *can* if you've got a name like Dolly Rider. Endless possibilities. Endless. Never underestimate the power of a name, Beatrice. Tell me, now, how old are you?"

"I'm fourteen, sir. And it's Dolly, actually. Dolly Rider. Sir."

Jesus fucking Christ. I hate actresses.

Arthur laughs and claps his hands together. "Brilliant, *brilliant*, you're already on your way, *Dolly*. Now, let's begin, yeah?"

TWO

STARS ON THE SIDEWALK

A S soon as she starts reciting the lines, I check out. I can't listen to them anymore. All the girls attempt to sound different, and in doing so, they all end up sounding exactly the same. It's Guantanamo-level torture. I stare out the rain-streaked window and try to calculate how much force it would take to break through if I hurled myself at it.

"Stop," Arthur says, cutting Beatrice (I can't—I *won't*—think of her as fucking Dolly) off midsentence. I look over at him. A flush has risen beneath the bronzed skin on his cheeks and neck. Sweat beads at his temples. To Tony, he says, "Leave us. Go out the side door, into the conference room. Don't go into the hall."

Tony, perplexed, looks questioningly at Arthur.

"Do it," Arthur commands. His tone leaves no window for compromise, but Tony still looks at me for some sort of affirmation, as if my input matters in any way. All I can do is nod. I know where this is going.

In earlier, bolder days, I'd privately cautioned Arthur against it, reminding him the climate has changed, and there are hashtags and women's movements to think about now. He'd given me a long, reproachful look and said, "I'm not afraid of hashtags, and I'm certainly not afraid of women. I'm too big to be brought down."

He was right. He's always right.

"Come on," I say to Tony, starting toward the door. "I'll get us some—"

"Not you, Ty," Arthur says to me. I cringe inwardly. "You stay."

He doesn't always make me watch.

Not always, but often.

• • •

Once Tony is gone, Arthur gets up and approaches Beatrice. He walks in a circle around her. Slow, appraising. "How badly," he says to her, "do you want this part?"

"Gosh," Beatrice says. "More than I've ever wanted anything, I guess."

"And what, dear girl, would you be willing to *do* in order to *get* it?"

She looks Arthur dead in the eyes and says, "I don't think there's much I wouldn't do, sir."

Something is wrong. Not, of course, in the traditional I'm-about-to-watch-an-underage-girl-perform-sexual-favors-in-order-to-get-a-part-in-a-shitty-commercial kind of sense. This is nothing unusual. This is status quo.

No, what's wrong is the girl's demeanor. Her composure. I've been present for dozens of these little transactions, and none of the girls were ever so ... so fucking *chill*. There's a faint air of apprehension about her—a barely perceptible trembling of the lip, a furtive darting of the eyes—but it's not enough, and I'm not even sure it's real. I think, maybe, she's acting.

"You can stop calling me 'sir' now," says Arthur.

• • •

I have to watch. If I don't watch—at least for the beginning, when he has enough wherewithal to pay attention to whether I'm paying attention— Arthur will berate me afterward. He might dock my pay, too, which is insubstantial enough as it is. It's not until he starts to get into it that I can look away, and even then, I have to make sure I look back when it's over.

Because of this, I have to watch as Beatrice undresses, and as the obscene bulge in my uncle's pants increases in size. I have to watch as she lies naked on the carpet, looking up at Arthur with big, doleful eyes.

"Touch your breasts," Arthur instructs her, and I have to watch as she obeys. I have to watch as he takes off his shoes and steps out of his pants and pulls down his underwear. When he tells her to finger her cunt, I have to watch that, too.

"Are you a virgin?" Arthur asks.

"Yes." There's authentic anxiety in her face now—still not enough, not nearly enough, but it's there, and it's real.

"Good. That's real good." Arthur's voice is hardly a whisper. "It'll hurt a bit, but try to enjoy it, yeah?"

I have to watch as he gets on the floor with her. I have to watch as she spreads her legs, a little too invitingly.

She whimpers when he enters her, and I have to watch as Arthur places his cupped hand over her mouth.

When he starts to thrust, though—that's when I look away.

I'm not watching, but I'm still here. I'm here in this room, in this city. I've spent my life getting here, and here I am. I can—and I do—tell myself I didn't know it would be like *this*, and on some level, maybe it's even true.

But on another level—a deeper, darker level—I did know.

I always knew.

My breath fogs the windowpane. For a moment, I let myself fantasize about disappearing into the fog, becoming the fog—nothing more than a formless, nameless, insignificant shape on a pane of glass—but only for a moment, because I can hear my uncle groaning through gritted teeth, and I have to turn back around.

Because I have to watch.

• • •

Arthur stands up, his cock limp and glistening. He looks at the naked girl on the floor, at the constellation of semen droplets drizzled across her stomach. "This is how I always want to remember you," he says. He mimes snapping a photograph. "Just like this."

"Remember me?" Beatrice asks. "Am I ... going somewhere?" I can't tell for sure if she's still acting, but I think she is. She's not dumb. She wants to appear dumb, but she's not dumb.

"The stars, Dolly, baby," says Arthur. "The stars on the sidewalk. Your name will be in fucking concrete if you play this shit right."

Dolly looks at her glazed stomach, seeming to ponder what she sees there. "Play what right?" she asks, looking back up at Arthur with her fawnlike eyes. "The part in the commercial?" She's definitely acting.

A thin trickle of blood is creeping out from between her legs. She touches two fingers to it and lifts them to her face, inspecting them with wide eyes. Her expression is something between horror and fascination, and I'm reasonably certain it's genuine.

"Baby, this commercial is only the beginning. That said, the part's yours, of course. My assistant here will get the necessary information from your mother and go through all the legal mumbo jumbo with you two." He pulls up his underwear and puts on his pants and shoes. "Oh, and there's a party on Friday night. It's at my house. I want you there, looking fabulous. I'll have Ty pick you up at eight."

"Okay," Beatrice says, with convincing meekness. "I'll have to check with my mom—"

"If your mom knows what's good for you, and thus good for *her*, she won't put up a fuss. You're in the big leagues now—"

Ha.

"—and you're gonna have to do big league shit." He winks at her. "And since you've already proven you're up to the task, I don't think you'll have any problems with what's next."

"Okay," Beatrice says again, with that same imitation sheepishness.

"Now, I'm going to go tell Tony we've found our star. Ty, get rid of the other girls and talk to Dolly's mother, yeah? Be charming. Just don't fuck her. Don't fuck *either* of them." He laughs. "Conflict of interest, and all that. Dolly, I'll see you Friday. Wear something slutty, but don't wear too much makeup. Don't cover up that youth."

• • •

Once Arthur is gone, Beatrice sits up slowly and looks at me, her face unreadable. I avert my eyes.

"It doesn't feel like I thought it would," she says.

"Yeah, well . . ." I clear my throat. "Most girls don't expect their first time to be . . . like that."

She's quiet for a moment, and I can feel her studying me. I wish she'd get dressed. I want to get out of here. "No. That's not what I mean," she says. "I was ready for *that*. My mom prepared me for it. She said if I ever got the chance to get a part on my back, or on my knees, to not hesitate." She pauses before adding, "I was hoping he'd just want a blowjob. I have more practice with that. My mom showed me how, with a dildo."

"That's kind of, um . . ." I search for the right word. I can't find it.

11

"I thought once I finally got a part in something, it would feel different than this. That's what I meant. I guess I expected to feel something. Anything."

She doesn't talk like a fourteen-year-old should. She doesn't even sound like the same girl who'd delivered those ridiculous lines. The saccharine obsequiousness is gone. There's a detached weariness to her voice. It doesn't fit.

"Why does he make you watch?"

The question catches me off guard. I look out the window. The rain has stopped. Spears of fading red sunlight pierce through the clouds.

"Is it because you're young and hot? I mean, he's not bad for his age. He's not fat or gross or anything. I always kind of expected my first time would be with a Harvey-type guy, so I guess it could have been way worse. But I can definitely tell he hates you. He hates you because you're pretty."

"He doesn't hate me. He's my uncle." I look at her. I've momentarily forgotten she's naked, and it startles me. The semen drying on her stomach makes me want to throw up. I walk over to the table and take the napkin out from beneath Tony's Diet Coke. "Here," I say, handing it to her. "Clean yourself up and get dressed."

"If he doesn't hate you, why does he make you watch him fuck young girls?"

To keep me in my place. To remind me of who he is, and who I'm not.

"It's . . . complicated."

"It doesn't seem that—"

"Get dressed," I say again. "Is your mother going to have any issue with you going to the party? I need to know if I'm walking into something that could get confrontational."

"God, no," she says, wiping herself off. She stands and starts putting on her clothes. "Her daughter, invited to a party at a rich producer's house? She'll be over the moon."

Over the moon. Not something you hear a lot of fourteen-year-olds say. The question is, why did she put on a front of dumb naivete for Arthur and Tony, but not for me? Does she see me as neutral ground, unthreatening, someone so insignificant she doesn't have to hide her true nature? Is it because I'm *just the assistant*?

"Okay," she says, stepping into her pumps. "I'm ready."

"One last thing. Your mother said something to you in the hallway before we came in."

Her mouth turns upward into a sad smile. Her eyes remain hard. "She said, 'Be confident, not cocky. Be sexy, not creepy.'"

THREE

A BEAUTIFUL LITTLE FOOL

ALLISON gets into my car, her cheerleading uniform wet and clinging from the rain. She pulls the sun visor down and inspects her reflection in the little rectangular mirror, tossing her black hair and inspecting her makeup. "Fucking rain," is all she says.

I ask her how practice went, not caring, pulling away from the high school and into traffic. A bus cuts me off, and I don't bother honking. Bus drivers in LA don't give a shit.

"It was whatever," says Allison. "I'm starving. Take me somewhere?"

I swallow and grip the steering wheel tighter, my fingers squeaking against the rubber. I want a cigarette, but I don't want to roll the window down because the rain might mess up my hair. "Where do you want to go?"

"Ummm. Somewhere close, I guess. The Henry?"

I do some calculations in my head. I could get the Green Garden

14

Kale salad for 310 calories, bringing me to a reasonably safe total of 470 for the day, but I got that last time and it might arouse suspicion. That means I'll have to get the Simple Raw Vegetable salad, which is 350 calories and would thus put me over 500, but if I get it without the parmesan I'd still be—

"Come on, Ty, *please*? I'm *hungry*." She smiles innocently at me, her braces gleaming. She's getting them taken off in a few months, a week before her seventeenth birthday, which will mostly be a tragedy. I kind of love the way my semen gets stuck in the brackets after she sucks me off.

I grumble my assent and punch the restaurant into my phone's GPS. Allison squeals and kisses me on the cheek.

I'm not dating a sixteen-year-old because it does something for my ego or anything like that. I'm not dating her because she has the body of a wet dream, or even for her insatiable sex drive. I'm certainly not dating her for her personality. I'm dating her because her father is a rich film financier, and I have *aspirations*. Granted, I don't think he'd be keen on bankrolling the passion project of a relatively poor, twenty-eight-year-old guy who's fucking his underage daughter, but I haven't worked out the particulars yet. All I know is working for my uncle isn't getting me anything but cuckolded, and I need to explore other avenues.

"You okay?" Allison asks. "You seem tense."

There's no way to tell her I'd been planning on having a vanilla Carbmaster yogurt for dinner—for a total of ninety calories—and she's ruined that for me, so I tell her I'm fine, long day, I'm just tired, but she's already on Instagram and doesn't hear me, so it doesn't matter.

Nothing matters.

I keep driving.

• • •

Most guys would be happy. This, I know. Most guys would be happy to be sitting here on a Tuesday night, on a plush leather couch in a hot sixteen-year-old's bedroom in her Bel Air mansion. They'd be happy to have said sixteen-year-old sprawled beside them in nothing but her bra and panties, her feet on their lap as she reads a copy of *The Great Gatsby*. They'd be happy to have shared a more-or-less pleasant dinner with her, answering her questions about what parties they've gone to lately and who, if anyone, has been reading their spec script. They'd be happy because her dad is out of town on business, and her stepmother is never home when her dad is gone, granting nigh-unlimited access to the sixteen-year-old's mansion and, thereby, the sixteen-year-old.

I know this. I'm supposed to be happy.

I am not happy.

"I don't get why I have to read this stupid book," says Allison. "I know it's a classic, or whatever, but I don't see why. It's just about rich people going to parties. I shouldn't have to waste my summer reading this junk. Whoever came up with summer reading lists has a special place in hell."

"You're too young," I say, sucking on her Juul because I'm not allowed to smoke inside the house. "They shouldn't assign it in high school. You haven't experienced enough."

She lays the book on her flat, tanned stomach and props herself up on her elbows, narrowing her eyes at me. "I'm not that young," she says. "I've experienced plenty."

"You have to have loved someone and lost them. You have to have seen that person with someone else. Until you know what that feels like, it's just a book about rich people going to parties."

She cocks her head, her expression softening. "Do *you* actually know what that feels like?"

I think of Judy and wait for a pang that never comes. It hasn't come in a long time. "Sort of," I say. "Not . . . totally. But enough to . . . get it. I can imagine what it feels like. I've gotten close to feeling it. I've gotten . . . very close."

"It's hard to imagine you loving anyone but yourself."

This isn't a test. I'm not supposed to say, "I love *you*, dear heart," or anything like that. That's not what this is. That's not what we are.

"I've gotten close," is all there is for me to say. Allison shrugs and picks the book back up. Dr. T.J. Eckleburg's mournful eyes stare into mine, as if saddened by what they don't see.

• • •

It takes me forty minutes to drive the sixteen miles from Allison's place to mine, which isn't terrible, but when I get there, I spend another twenty-five minutes looking for parking. I drive around in circles, screaming and punching the roof of my car and slamming my head into the steering wheel, pleading with an absent god for a break I know I'm not going to get. I finally settle for a narrow space on El Centro, about three blocks from my building. The rain is coming down hard, and I'm cold and soaked and still out of breath from screaming by the time I've completed the trek.

When I let myself into my tiny apartment—I spent a few hours in a jail cell as a teenager, and it had been spacious by comparison—I turn on the lights, sending the cockroaches skittering for the cracks where the floor meets the wall. My stomach rumbles, and I glance at the mini-fridge in the corner. I hate myself for the longing I feel. I am ashamed of it, sickened by it.

I stand on my desk chair and unscrew the smoke detector. Lighting a cigarette, I collapse onto my faux leather futon and check my phone. There's a text from Arthur, asking if everything went okay with "Dolly's" mother and if she'll be at the party. I respond and tell him everything went fine, and she'll be there. After thinking for a few moments, I send another text saying, *It isn't going to be like last time, is it?*

A couple of minutes pass, and then he responds, *no. not exactly.*

Not exactly. I could ask for clarification, but he'd get annoyed. I don't know why I care. She's just a dumb actress.

He hates you because you're pretty.

I shut off the lights and wait for the yellow woman to come.

FOUR

BETTER THAN DEMONS

WHEN I was in film school at USC, and for a time shortly after, I dated a poetry major named Judy Coover who told me about demons.

"I see them sometimes, in people's faces," she said to me one night as she was doing her makeup in her costume vanity mirror. "It's weird, it's like a . . . it's just, like, the slightest *shift* in their features, you feel me? It's like everything kind of *slides* so it's not quite right. And it's awful. It's the most awful, awful thing, and I see it all the time. Sometimes, I even see it in myself."

I was sitting on her bed, smoking a cigarette and leafing through her battered copy of *Arthur Rimbaud: Complete Works*. Hole's "Softer, Softest" was playing low on her stereo. I looked up at her. "Do you ever see it in me?" I asked.

She paused in the application of her blush and swiveled on her chair to regard me with a sober stare. "Yes," she said. "*Especially* you. I see it in you most of all."

The small room was shadowy, with the only light coming from the bulbs dotted around her mirror, and I felt my eyes drift to the dark corner near her closet. The yellow woman was there, I was sure of it, just beyond the reaches of vision. Watching me. Waiting for me.

I swallowed and looked away. Judy resumed her ritual.

"What do you think it means?" I asked, not wanting her to answer.

She shrugged and uncapped a tube of lipstick, leaning forward and pursing her lips in the mirror. "I think," she said, "that everyone is haunted by something. I'd even go so far as to say that everyone is *possessed*, actually. Or, rather . . . well, let's say, everyone is in a state of . . . *pre*-possession, I guess. We all have these demons, right? Living inside of us, *waiting* for the opportunity to take over. And, of course, it's nothing biblical or *Exorcist*-y, or anything like that. It's just, you know, our own *issues*, or whatever. When you hear about demonic possession happening, it's not a case of some foreign entity *getting* in us, because it's *already* in us, it's always *been* in us. No, it's a case of the worst parts of ourselves—things we've done, or things that were done *to* us—taking over the best parts of ourselves."

I could have sworn I saw a flash of excited movement from the corner, and I flinched.

"How do you beat it?" I asked distantly, eyeing the shadows in the corner, monitoring for more movement.

"It's easy," Judy said, her voice flippant. "You have to be better than the demons that haunt you. You always have to be better." She took a brush from one of her drawers and began running it through her rolling waves of wild black hair. I loved her hair. I didn't love her.

"What if you can't be better?"

Judy looked over her shoulder at me as she continued to weave the brush through her hair. I met her gaze, and I wished she could be enough. "Then they will define you," she said. "And they will consume you."

FIVE

ANOTHER UNREACHABLE ITCH

O N Friday night, after spending about an hour getting ready— combing and recombing my hair, shaving twice, tweezing my eyebrows, trimming my nostrils and ears, trying various clothing en- sembles, spritzing on a modest application of cologne, and recombing my hair again—I drive to the address Beatrice's mother, Francesca, had given me. I arrive at quarter after eight. It's a big Tudor house in a clean, quiet neighborhood in San Marino, just southeast of Pasadena. I'm guessing Mr. Rider is a lawyer or a doctor, or something.

I've not eaten today, so I'm feeling pretty good as I walk to the front door, if a little weak. Francesca opens the door almost as soon as I ring the doorbell. She looks more attractive than I remember her looking on Tuesday. Younger, fresher, tanner. Smartly attired in a suggestively cut silk evening dress that seems too fancy for an evening at home. I'm won- dering if it's for my benefit as she welcomes me inside, and I realize how much she looks like her daughter.

"Dolly should be down any minute," Francesca says, guiding me into the living room. I recoil at her use of my uncle's pet name for Beatrice.

"Dolly?" I say, looking around at the quaint suburban furnishings.

"Yes, yes, she told me it was your idea. A *lovely* idea, if I might say so. Very showbizzy." She looks over her shoulder and calls into the kitchen, somewhat shrilly, "*ERIC. MR. SEWARD IS HERE, COME SAY HELLO.*" To me, in a much more subdued tone, she says, "Can I get you anything, Mr. Seward? Some scotch, perhaps? Some brandy?"

"I'm okay, thanks." I can smell whiskey on her breath, and I'm not buying the squeaky-clean housewife role she's playing. Her daughter is a better actress.

A man, presumably Eric, enters holding two tumblers of liquor. He hands one to his wife and shakes my hand. "Eric Rider," he says gruffly. He's older than Francesca, maybe early forties, with gray in his temples. I can't tell if his grim, no-nonsense demeanor is part of the Protective Dad routine, or if he's simply worn down.

"Honey, *darling*," Francesca drawls to her husband. She's drunker than I thought. She downs the whiskey with a single swallow and says, "Mr. Seward is one of the producers on the commercial."

"Yes. So you said." Eric scrutinizes my face, as if he's looking for something that might betray my true nature.

"You can just call me Ty," I say, shifting from one foot to the other and trying to smile. I don't correct Francesca; "producer" sounds a lot better than "assistant."

"Well, Ty, I've gotta say I'm not crazy about my daughter going to a Hollywood party that I know nothing about."

I laugh uneasily, hoping it sounds good-natured. "It's not what you think," I say, not lying. "It's not like it is in the movies."

"Well, I should hope not."

If only he knew.

"You will, I trust, have her home by midnight."

"Oh, *darling*," says Francesca, swatting her husband's arm. "Don't be *ridiculous*."

"I'm not being ridiculous. She's fourteen. There's no reason for her to be out past midnight. Actually, I think I'm being generous here."

Francesca rolls her eyes. "Oh, *yes*, how *big* of you. She has to grow up sometime, Eric. She's an actress now. She has a *part*. Let her mingle with the elite." She thrusts her glass at him. "Now, be a doll and freshen me up, will you?"

Eric looks at the glass, but doesn't take it. "Frankly," he says, "I don't like the idea of her *mingling* with the *elite*. I've seen the headlines. I've read the stories. The elite are the ones we need to be worried about." He casts a wary glance at me. Maybe I should have corrected Francesca, after all.

"That's absurd," scoffs Francesca. "What are you worried about? That some rich movie producer is going to fuck her? Is *that* what this is about? Would you be *jealous*? I know *I* would be, but I'm certainly not going to interfere with our daughter's career just because I'm envious that other people get to fuck her and I don't."

"Maybe I should . . . wait outside," I say.

"Ignore her," Eric says, his jaw clenched. "She's trying to get a reaction out of me. She's fucked in the head."

"Oh, get off your high horse," says Francesca. "Don't pretend like you don't want to fuck her, too."

"You're sick."

"That's quite rich, coming from the man who keeps fucking younger and younger women. Have you considered, perhaps, that you're subconsciously trying to get closer to filling a surrogate void because you can't fill the one that's between your daughter's legs?"

"Are you even hearing yourself?"

"Jesus, Eric. Are *you* hearing *yourself*? Am I the only one who's been paying *any* attention to what you've been doing for the last however many years? Are you even *conscious* when you fuck those girls? I'm sure *they* aren't, but are *you*? Why do you do it, if not out of some misbegotten attempt to scratch that unreachable place on your back?"

"Really," I say, tugging at my collar and scratching my neck, "I can wait outside. Totally not a big deal."

Neither of them appears to have heard me. Eric stares into the depths of his drink. "Your problem," he says to his wife in a disarmingly soft tone, "is that you view the world through a lens where everyone is just as twisted as you are. Honestly, you're reading way too much into things. There's no weird Oedipal motivation behind the things I've done."

"That's not how an Oedipus complex works. You have the roles confused. You'd know that if you hadn't made me do your assignments for you in college."

"I never made you do anything. Whatever. That's not the point."

"Then *what*, pray tell, *is* the point?" She glares at him, raising her eyebrows.

He starts to raise his glass toward his mouth, his hand trembling, the ice rattling, but then he lowers it and says, "The point is that I can't deal with you. You're too much. Nothing is enough for you. You wanted a child *so fucking badly*, and I gave you one, and it wasn't enough. Then, you wanted a big house in Villa Vida, so I gave you that, and *that* wasn't enough. Now, we're out here in fucking Los Angeles so the daughter you wanted *so fucking badly* can be a movie star, and you're still miserable. When will it ever be enough?"

"Well, excuse me for wanting a husband who doesn't sleep with other women. I hadn't realized that was too much to ask."

"And excuse *me* for wanting a woman who will shut up and fuck me every once in a while. I *did* realize that was too much to ask, so I went elsewhere."

I look toward the stairs, hoping Beatrice will materialize and rescue me, but no such miracle occurs.

"Listen," says Eric. "This has gone way off the rails. This is about our daughter. The one *you* wanted. You need to be a mother to her. Whatever you have to do in order to put your issues with me aside so you can help me raise our daughter right, then fucking do it. Hell, fuck someone else, if you think that'll help. A dude, a chick, the fucking pool boy—I don't give a damn. I don't know how to make this marriage work. I don't know how *any* marriage works, honestly, but maybe that's the ticket. Maybe monogamy is a dying concept. Maybe it's already dead."

"Hm. Maybe. Would that make you happy? If I fucked someone else? Would it assuage your guilt?"

Eric shuts his eyes and massages the bridge of his nose with his thumb and forefinger. "Here's the thing, Fran. I don't feel guilty. I used to, but not anymore. Like I said, do what you have to do. I don't care. I just care that our daughter gets taken care of."

"Trust me, I don't think *that's* something you have to worry about."

"Fucking hell. You're an impossible cunt." He turns to me, his eyes weary but hostile and narrowed. "If anything happens to her, I'll kill you." He exits the room, his shoulders hunched and his head hanging.

"*Well*," says Francesca, smiling innocuously and fanning her face with her hand. "I *am* sorry about *that*."

I'm about to ask if I could have the drink she'd offered, after all, when Beatrice appears. She's taken Arthur's instructions to heart, wearing a short, low-cut red dress and black leather stiletto boots that go up to her knees. Her lightly applied makeup is the only tasteful thing about her getup, which makes the whole ensemble even more scandalous.

"See what I *mean*?" Francesca whispers to me, clutching my arm. "How could you *not* want to fuck her?"

"We should be going," I say, looking at my watch.

"Yes, yes, of course," says Francesca. "And please, don't pay any mind to my husband. He's a bit overprotective, is all. Keep her out as late as necessary. Hell, keep her all night, if you have to." She winks at me.

My stomach flips.

• • •

Walking to the car, Beatrice says, "What did my mom whisper to you?"

I light a cigarette and say, "She said you look very nice."

SIX
DEAD FLOWERS

WE'RE both silent for the beginning of the drive. It's not until I turn onto the 110 that I say, "Why did you tell your mother I gave you the stage name?"

She doesn't answer at first. She looks out the window, at the lights and the palm trees. With her face angled away, dressed like she is, I have to remind myself of her age. "I don't know," she says. "I guess I just didn't want to talk about Arthur any more than I had to."

"Right." I think about my words, choosing them with careful deliberation. I'm not good at things like this. Sentimentality is beyond my reach. "Listen—um, I'm . . . I'm sorry. About that. About . . . what he did. To you. It's . . . not right. It's very . . . wrong."

She responds with a cold, harsh laugh. It's a grownup sound, and it unnerves me. "I don't know why you're sorry. I'm not a *victim*. I knew what I was doing. I had a choice, and I made it. I could have walked out. I wasn't tied down." She lets the words hang there. The silence grows between us, flexing and pulsating. I change lanes and light another cigarette. "I don't want to be an actress," she says. "Not really."

"Could have fooled me," I snort. It sounds crueler than I'd intended, so I add, "It just seems . . . you seem very committed."

"Have you *met* my mother?"

I frown. "So . . . it's all just to please her?"

She reaches into my center console and takes out my pack of L&Ms and my lighter. Rolling her window down, she lights one with casual expertise. "Mostly, I guess. But I want to believe that when I achieve all the things she wants me to achieve, I'll feel . . . I don't know. Fulfilled."

"Don't buy into that. There's no fulfillment in acting. Actors are the most miserable, parasitic people on the planet. They're disgusting. You don't want to be one of them."

"You work in kind of a weird business for someone who hates actors so much."

"Yeah, well. I have aspirations."

"Well, I guess I sort of do, too. Like, in a roundabout way. And things are starting to, you know, happen."

"This commercial," I say hesitantly, "you have to understand. It's not a big thing. I know Arthur made it sound—"

"You don't have to explain it to me. I'm not an idiot. I know it's not a 'big break,' or whatever. But it's something. It's the first thing I've gotten. My mother is very pleased."

I don't ask her if her mother knows how she got it. I don't want to know.

"I guess I—" She pauses. I can feel her looking at me. Knowing what she's looking at, I tense up and don't look at her. She reaches out and gingerly touches the side of my neck. "You have a scar," she says. "I didn't notice it before." Withdrawing her hand, she says, "What's it from?"

I consider lying as I turn onto the 101, but it seems like more effort than it's worth. "Cancer," I say. "It was cancer. There was a tumor. They took it out, but not in time."

"Not in time? What do you mean?"

I sigh, not wanting to get into it, but feeling compelled to, for some reason. "By the time they took the tumor out, the cancer had already spread. The prognosis, it was ... grim. I got some second and third opinions, but everything pointed to radiation, so that's what I did. Very radical, very intensive. Things were pretty touch-and-go for a while. I don't think anyone expected me to make it. I didn't expect to make it."

"Whoa. Criminy. When was this?"

"Almost five years ago. Winter, 2015. I spent New Year's Eve in a hospital bed at USC. I had a bad reaction to the radiation. It had made it impossible for me to swallow, so I had to be hospitalized for about a week so the doctors could pump me with fluids and monitor my vitals. I was lying there on New Year's Eve, surrounded by flowers, waiting to die. I wished I would. That was all I wanted. I wanted it all to be over. The sickness, the pain, the uncertainty—it was all too much." I suck hard on the cigarette. I don't know why I'm telling her all this.

"Criminy," Beatrice says again.

"I've hated flowers ever since. There were so many goddamn flowers in that awful little room. Everyone sent them. Every flower you can imagine. I watched them all die. Every last one of them wilted and fell apart and died, but I lived."

Beatrice touches my arm, and I jump a little. "Well, um . . . I'm glad you did," she says. "Like, they got it, right? You're cured? Or, like . . . in remission, or whatever?"

I shrug, jetting around a lagging BMW. "Sure, for now. But the cancer I had—it has a fifty percent recurrence rate. I don't think it's really gone. It's asleep. It's waiting. My life is nothing more than a coin toss."

"I mean, isn't everyone's?"

"Not like mine is."

She stares hard at me through the curling tendrils of cigarette smoke. "What makes you so different? Anyone could step outside and get hit by a—"

"By a bus, right, I've heard that one before." I flick my cigarette out the window, watching in the reflection of the driver's side mirror as it hits the asphalt in an explosion of embers. "It's different when the bus feels like an inevitability. And a bus would be quick."

"But you don't know for *sure* that you're going to get hit by the bus."

"I do, though. I can feel it." A chill creeps along my spine as I utter the words, and my eyes go to the rearview mirror. I expect to see the yellow woman leering at me from the back seat, and I'm relieved to find she isn't.

For now, at least.

She's never far away.

SEVEN
THE ELITE

"**W**ELCOME to Casa de Doctor Law," I grumble as I turn off Mulholland Dr. and roll through the gate into Arthur's enormous compound. I join the line of cars waiting for the valet. My Camry looks obscene and out of place among the Rolls-Royces and Ferraris and Range Rovers. My economic dysphoria is at full-tilt.

"Who's Doctor Law?" Beatrice asks, looking wide-eyed out the window at the palatial scenery of the grounds—the statues, the gardens, the fountains, the rooftop helipad.

"Arthur. It's what people call him. He was a doctor, at one point in his life. Then he was a lawyer. Now, he's . . ." I struggle to find the right word.

"A producer?" Beatrice regards me with raised eyebrows, as if I've suddenly gone retarded.

I shake my head. "No, that's just a front. He's something . . . else."

She starts to press the issue, but then a valet in a red tuxedo is opening my door. "Mr. Seward," he says, bowing slightly. "I am sorry about the wait."

"It's fine, Javier," I say, about forty percent certain I got his name right. I catch him casting an uneasy glance at Beatrice. "She'll be fine," I tell him, tipping him a dollar. I think about it and reluctantly hand him a second one, sighing.

He nods and thanks me, noticeably embarrassed that I sensed his distress over Beatrice's presence. Arthur's staff are paid exorbitant salaries to turn a blind eye to the goings-on at his house—more than *I* make, I realize, regretting the second dollar—and they're not supposed to have opinions about my uncle's unsavory business practices.

"Is everything okay?" Beatrice asks once the valet has driven my car off to the underground parking structure. "I feel like he looked at me funny."

"Everything is fine," I say, putting my hand on her back and leading her to the front door. "He probably just . . . liked your dress."

• • •

My Aunt Carlotta greets us in the foyer. She's holding a daiquiri in that way rich women hold their drinks. "Tyler, darling," she says, air-kissing me. "So glad you made it. And *who* is *this*?"

"Dolly Rider," Beatrice says, shaking Carlotta's hand. I can see the younger girl appraising the older one, taking her in, judging her.

Carlotta is the kind of woman who might have been pretty at some point in her life, but the facelifts and Botox and artificial sun have made her look like a poorly embalmed corpse. I guess it's no wonder my uncle goes elsewhere to get his needs met.

Aunt Carlotta releases Beatrice's hand and gently touches her cheek. "My, *my*, Tyler. I know you like them young, but . . . *well*." Her lips curl into a nasty smile and she shakes her head, not disapprovingly.

"Arthur wanted me to bring her," I say, a little too defensively. "He just cast her in a commercial." I search her face for a reaction, hoping she's been smarted by the implications of this. I don't know why because I don't exactly have any real problem with her other than the fact that she's annoying. In any case, it doesn't matter—if she's bothered by the idea of Arthur inviting this Pretty Young Thing to their house, it isn't evident in her unmoving, Plasticine-esque face.

"You have a lovely home, ma'am," Beatrice says, her voice sweet and childlike. How smoothly she slips back into that façade. It's unsettling.

"You're very sweet, dear," says Carlotta. I hear more guests entering behind us, and Carlotta waves at them. "Tyler, darling, be a good boy and go get yourselves something to drink at the bar. Mingle, have fun. Arthur will be getting into his—" she glances at Beatrice "—well, his *usual business* any time now, so best you enjoy yourselves until then."

• • •

Sitting at the bar, nursing a scotch (only about 100 calories, so I can afford to have this and three more before getting uncomfortable) while Beatrice sips her martini, I'm waiting for the question when it comes. I'm still not ready for it.

"What did your aunt mean?" she asks, looking at me with shrewd eyes. She isn't holding the glass right. I reach out and correct her wrist.

Wishing I could smoke in here, I look around at the rich people staring at shit on their phones—probably Instagram—and mumbling to each other about Rich People Nonsense. I should be right there with them, complaining about the help and boasting about yachts and the latest Learjet amenities. Instead, I'm just close enough to taste it, to smell it, ever on the periphery.

"Ty? What's his 'usual business'?"

"It's nothing. With any luck, you won't have to find out."

A girl in a bikini comes over to us, holding a silver platter arranged with lines of coke. She holds out a crystal tube. I take it and do a line. When I hand the tube back, she offers it to Beatrice. Beatrice looks at me, unsure. I shrug and don't say anything. She takes the tube and does a line. It isn't graceful, but it's efficient enough. Her eyes begin to water as soon as she lifts her head. A sloppy smile breaks out across her face, making her look years younger than she already does. She bends back down and does another line.

"That's enough," I say, plucking the tube from her fingers and giving it back to the girl in the bikini, who takes it wordlessly and struts away. "Letting you OD on blow isn't going to get me into your dad's good graces."

Still smiling that goofy smile, she puts her hand on my thigh and says, "Why do *you* care what my dad thinks of you?" She sniffs and squeezes my leg.

I look at her hand. I move it away. "I'm responsible for you," I say. "You're under my watch."

"*Aww*, that's so *cute*." She sniffs again. "You know, you should really–" She grimaces, swallows, and makes a noise halfway between a cough and a gag.

"Drink," I say. "It'll help with the drip." She does as I say, tilting the glass back and draining half its contents. "Easy, easy. Not so much."

She coughs again and gives a vigorous little shake of her head. "*That*," she says, "is unpleasant."

"All good things come with something horrible." I shrug. "It's worth it."

"No arguments *there*. Now, you were about to tell me–"

"About to tell you *what*?" says Arthur, seeming to appear out of thin air, as if conjured like the devil he is. He takes Beatrice's hand and kisses it. "My darling, you look absolutely ravishing. Flat-out *stunning*. You're a star if I ever saw one, and I've seen a few."

"Oh my *gosh*, that's so *nice*," says Beatrice. Knowing she's acting doesn't make her schtick any less grating. "Ty was about to tell me . . . um . . . how you and Carlotta met." She smiles. She sniffs.

"Yeah?" Arthur raises an eyebrow. "Funny, *I* don't even remember how we met." He looks at me. "But Ty always did have a knack for remembering useless bullshit." Laughing, he slaps me hard on the back.

"Ty, a word?" He takes my arm and leads me to an unoccupied corner of the room. I'm ready for him to scold me about whatever he thought I'd been "about" to tell Beatrice, but he already seems to have forgotten about that. "Listen, Ty," he begins eagerly, breathlessly. "The main event starts in—" he glances at his Rolex "—thirty minutes. Only a select group has been invited, of course. I want you and Dolly there. Make sure she pays attention, yeah? Make sure she watches *the whole thing*."

I sigh, looking at my shoes and running a hand through my hair. "Right," I say. "Uh. Look. Don't you think—"

"Don't I think *what*, Ty?" He grips my shoulder and leans in close to my face. He's like a caricature of a cokehead—the eyes darting back and forth so fast they seem to be vibrating, the clenching and unclenching jaw, the forehead slick with perspiration. He sniffs.

Not meeting his eyes, I say, "It just seems . . . soon. You've never made any of the other girls watch this early."

"Haven't I? Well, it doesn't matter. She's special."

"What's special about her?"

His bloodshot eyes bulge. "Shit, man, *look* at her. That body. That face. Those *legs*." He leans in closer, whispering in my ear, "Her pussy felt like home, Ty. It was a dream. It was the most wonderful dream."

"I, ah, I don't . . . doubt it."

"I licked her pussy-blood from my underwear." He shudders. "You wouldn't understand."

"No. I guess I wouldn't."

"I haven't washed my dick all week. I cover it in Saran wrap every time I shower."

"That . . . doesn't sound sanitary."

He pulls away, patting my shoulder. "Make sure she watches, yeah? The whole thing."

EIGHT

SEX AND DYING IN HIGH SOCIETY

"TY," Beatrice whispers, tugging at my sleeve. "What is this?"

We're standing with about a dozen other party guests—all of them male, mostly producers and studio executives, but also a few well-known actors whom I can only hope Beatrice doesn't recognize—in a vast room in Arthur's mansion. The lights are dimmed low. The walls and floor are covered in plastic tarpaulin. In the middle of the room is a metal gurney with a naked boy strapped to it. He's probably a couple of years younger than Beatrice. Standing on either side of the gurney is a teenage boy in a speedo, their postures rigid, their faces slack. They have erections.

Arthur emerges from a door on the other side of the room. He comes to stand in front of the gurney, rubbing his hands together. "Gentlemen," he says, "I know you're eager to get started, so I won't waste any time. Let's start the bidding at ten thousand dollars, yeah?"

The men start calling out figures. Their voices are calm, their faces stoic.

"I hear fourteen thousand," says Arthur. "Do I hear fifteen?"

"*Ty*," Beatrice whispers to me again. "What *is* this?"

"Eighteen thousand, can I get nineteen?"

"This," I whisper to her, "is capitalism."

Someone says, "Twenty-five thousand."

Someone else says, "Thirty thousand."

"*Ty*," says Beatrice, hysteria creeping into her voice. "What are they going to do to that boy?"

"No matter what happens, don't look away. Arthur was adamant about that. You have to watch the whole thing."

"Forty thousand going once."

"Ty, are they going to *hurt* him?"

"Forty thousand going twice."

"Just watch."

"*Sold.*"

One of the studio executives steps forward, smiling. Everyone else applauds with quiet golf claps. The executive shakes Arthur's hand and begins to undress.

The guy next to me has his hand in the pocket of his pants and is pleasuring himself. Beatrice notices this and makes a face.

"Don't look away," I tell her.

Naked, the executive gets on his knees at the foot of the gurney. He

the boy. His fists make loud, wet sounds when they slap against the boy's blood-and-semen-coated face. Blood patters onto the clear plastic. This goes on for a minute or two, and then the executive leans down and bites the boy's mouth. The boy screams as the executive tears off his upper lip, chewing it for a moment before spitting it onto the floor. The executive digs his thumbs into the boy's eyes and gouges until both eyeballs hang down onto his cheeks from ropy stalks.

Beatrice squeezes my hand tighter.

The executive dismounts from the writhing and screaming boy. He returns to the foot of the gurney and starts pulling and twisting on the boy's testicles. Another thin spurt of shit slickens the executive's wrist right before the boy's scrotum comes off. Blood gets everywhere. The executive places the fleshy sack in his mouth. He's hard again, and he inserts his cock into the hole he's created and starts thrusting. He comes almost immediately, his face pinched and the muscles in his neck taut. There's more applause. The executive beams triumphantly, bowing low.

After that, the crowd starts to disperse. Some of them approach the executive, congratulating him and shaking his hand even though it's still covered in shit and blood, or maybe because of it. Beatrice lets go of my own hand and bolts for the door, pushing past people who regard her with politely bemused smiles. I follow her, calling out her name. She looks over her shoulder at me, her eyes red with tears, but she doesn't stop. I pursue her through the house, walking briskly through the kitchen, the dining room, the parlor, the billiards room. I muse to myself, absurdly, about how impressive it is that she can move so quickly in those heels. She doesn't slow until she reaches an automatic sliding glass door that lets her out into the pool area. She stops at the edge of the infinity pool, looking out over the hills below, and at the glittering lights of downtown Los Angeles in the distance. I come up beside her, looking around. There is, thankfully, no one else out here. I light a cigarette, offer her one. She takes it without a word of acknowledgment.

"*Why?*" she breathes after a minute or two of unbearable silence. "Why did you make me watch that?"

"I didn't want to. It wasn't me. It was Arthur. He . . . made me."

Beatrice looks up at me, her sodden eyes full of reproach. "He can't make you do anything. Did he, like, hold a gun to your head? Because, if not, I don't see—"

"It's not that simple. You don't . . . You don't know how powerful he is. You don't know what he can do. What you just saw—that's not even the half of it."

"So, why don't you *quit*? Just because he's your uncle doesn't mean you *have* to work for him."

"Like I said, it's not that simple. You can't cut ties with Doctor Law. He's bigger than anyone in this town. He has his hands in everything, fucking everything." I pause, hitting my cigarette hard. "He also paid for my medical treatments. Every last one of them. In full, out of his own pocket."

Beatrice makes a face. "Well, that's great and all, but it was the decent thing to do. I mean, look at all this." She spreads her arms out, gesturing at the opulent scenery. "He has more money than God. Seriously, paying for you to get better was the least he could do."

"If he hadn't helped me, I would have been fucked. Totally fucked. It was hundreds of thousands of dollars, and I don't have insurance. I still don't. That's another piece of it. I have to get yearly PET scans, to make sure it hasn't come back. Those aren't cheap, and he pays for all of them."

"Yeah, well, he should, like I said. People who are well-off are supposed to help the people who aren't."

I look out at the city, so beautiful and bright, so strange. So ugly and terrible. In a voice sounding far away, I ask, "Are they, though?"

"Yeah, they are." She drags from her cigarette. "You know, you can't live in his shadow forever."

In the distance, a flashing neon sign proclaims, "FAME IS FLEETING. PERFECTION IS FOREVER." Staring at the sign, I say, "Whether you know it or not, we all live in his shadow. Everyone in this city is under his domain."

"I think you're giving him more credit than he deserves. He's just another rich asshole. This town is full of them."

"You don't get it. He's much more than that."

She shrugs. "Whatever. I still don't see why it was so important to him for me to watch."

I look at her. She is, I decide, extraordinarily beautiful. I hadn't noticed it that day in the casting office; she'd looked as most LA girls look—blonde, pretty, conceited, more than a little flighty, too aware of the effect she has on men. Beatrice's real beauty is something darker, more ominous. It lurks beneath the veneer of her casual Californian good looks. It's something that grows on you. Maybe it's her hidden intelligence—that wry, precocious, world-weary wit she masks so well when she needs to—that's allowed me to see it. Maybe it's how she looks in that dress. I swallow, reminding myself of how young she is. I look away.

"I don't know what he gets out of it," I say. "You're not the only girl he's subjected to something like that. I think it's . . . I really don't know. Maybe it's some sort of power trip. Who knows. It's . . . probably best not to psychoanalyze Arthur."

"He's not that complicated. He thinks he's so smart, but he's really not. Like, the whole 'Dolly' thing? Come on. I read *Lolita*. I knew right away he was being lewd. I honestly would have preferred Margot, though, because I think *Laughter in the Dark* is a way better book."

"I . . . haven't read it," I admit, feeling somewhat abashed.

"You should. It's one of Nabokov's best, next to *Ada, or Ardor*."

"You're . . . really very smart."

She looks at me sideways and snorts. "Do you use dumb lines like that on all the girls?"

I look away, my cheeks burning.

"Relax, it's whatever. Anyway, I'm not that smart." She sighs, exhaling smoke from her nostrils as she does. "I've just read a lot of books, I guess. My mom made me read them. She said it would make me a better actress."

"She's probably right." I see her cigarette is nearly out, so I take it from her. I carry it over to a potted plant by one of the chaise lounges and deposit it, along with my own cigarette butt, into the soil. When I return to her, I ask, "Have you read any Shakespeare?"

"Some, not a ton. Like, the main ones, I guess."

"My dream is to direct a completely faithful adaptation of *Romeo and Juliet*. I've already written the script. It's not framed as a love story, the way the movies always are. Mine is much more of a social drama. The two leads are exactly as Shakespeare wrote them—young and stupid and selfish, blinded by lust, enslaved to their family dynamics. None of that star-crossed lover bullshit. It's dark and nihilistic, like Polanski's *Macbeth*."

"I don't think a whole lot of people would pay to see that. No offense."

I shrug. "Neither does anyone I've pitched it to. And they all think my script is too long."

"How long is it?"

"Two hundred and thirty-six pages."

"Criminy." She laughs quietly. "You know scripts are supposed to be under a hundred pages, right? That's, like, Screenwriting 101."

"Yes. But this is a masterpiece."

"Oh, brother. You know, I kind of like you. Don't ruin that by turning out to be some douchey art-bro."

I clear my throat. "We should . . . go back inside."

"Give me another cigarette," she says, holding out her hand. "I need another few minutes to get my bearings. I'll meet you in there."

I hesitate for a moment before handing her a cigarette and lighting it for her. When I go inside, I have to resist the urge to glance back at her.

• • •

Almost as soon as I walk through the sliding glass door, I'm accosted by Les, Lex, and Len—identical triplets who make up Frisk, a boy band that had been mega popular in the early- to mid-2000s. They still put an album out every few years, but their fame has faded. I've never liked them. They creep me out, and the rumors that the three of them have an incestuous relationship were never quite hard enough for me to believe. Still, they're always around. Arthur doesn't particularly like them, either, but Carlotta is a huge fan of their music, and she finds their forthright flamboyance charming.

You can only tell them apart by the manner in which they style their white-blond hair. Les wears it long and poofy, like an '80s glam rocker. Lex keeps his cropped short. Len has a pixie cut that wouldn't be out of place on a thirty-something suburban housewife demanding to speak to a manager.

"Hey, babesy," says Les, pulling me into a too-tight hug. I don't return the embrace, and my muscles go rigid at his touch. The women's perfume he's wearing is strong enough to choke on. "It's been *way* too long."

"I think it's only been a couple of weeks."

"*Exactly* my *point*, babes." He releases me and pinches my cheek. "Now, what were you *doing* out there, hanging out all by your *lonesome*? A birdy told us you left Arthur's little show in an *awfully* big hurry."

"I wasn't alone," I say, but immediately regret it. I'd like to avoid exposing Beatrice to these creeps if at all possible.

"There's no shame if you were," says Lex. "We were going to come keep you company."

"For old times' sake," adds Len. He's grinning, but his voice is flat.

I flinch, looking at Len confusedly. "For—Wait, what? What are you . . . talking about?"

"Oh, *babesy*," says Les, stepping closer to me. "Don't play *coy*." He grabs my crotch. I recoil, shoving his hand away.

"Cool it," I say. "Enough."

"Oh, come *on*," says Les. "I always behave myself so *well* around you. I think I've earned the right to get a *little* handsy, don't *you*?"

"For old times' sake," says Len again.

I glare at Len and say, "Seriously, man, what is your *deal*?"

"Pretty soon, you're gonna be too old for us," says Lex.

"You of all people know how young we like them," says Len.

"Is that supposed to mean something?"

"It can *mean* whatever you *want* it to *mean*, babesy," says Les.

"Look, not that this hasn't been great, but I really need to—"

I hear the automatic glass door open behind me, and I'm both relieved and distraught to see Beatrice appear beside me. "Am I interrupting something?" she says.

"*Well*, my *stars*," says Les, bending down with his hands on his knees so he can look Beatrice directly in the face. "Aren't *you* just the *prettiest*." He winks up at me and says, "You didn't *tell* us you brought a *date*."

"No wonder Ty's so standoffish tonight," says Lex.

"He's pussy-struck," says Len.

"It's not like that," I say.

All three of them titter like women at a hair salon. Les stands and pats my face, saying, "It never is, babesy, it never is." I swat his hand away.

"Ty, I want another drink," whines Beatrice, taking hold of my wrist. She's coolly reverted back to her childish ruse. Even the light in her eyes seems dimmer. I think she might actually go places. "I don't remember where the bar is. Will you take me?"

"Better listen to the young lady," says Lex. "Wouldn't want to keep her waiting. You might not get any later, if you do."

"Not from her," says Len, licking his lips.

"No *fair*," says Les, pouting and stamping his foot. "We were *just* about to go for a *swim*, and we were *going* to invite you to join us."

"We don't have bathing suits," says Len.

"Terribly sorry I'll have to miss that," I say.

"Oh, babesy, I *know* you are," says Les. "You know where to find us if you change your mind." At that, the three of them exit out the sliding glass door. Les smacks my ass as he passes.

"Wow," Beatrice says when they're gone. "Those guys suck."

"Come on," I say. "Let's get you that drink."

NINE

FILLING A VOID

O N the way back, in the uncomfortable silence of the car, I ask Beatrice where she's originally from. "Your parents were . . . arguing. Before you came down. Your dad said something about a big house somewhere, something with a V, before coming to LA."

"Villa Vida," Beatrice says. "It's a suburb of Cleveland."

"Ohio?"

"Is there another Cleveland?"

"There's one in Tennessee," I say, momentarily impressed with myself that I know this and she doesn't. Then I remember she's fourteen, and I am ashamed.

"Oh. Well, yeah, Ohio."

"When did you come out here?"

"Like, a little over a year ago. My grandpa died and left my dad a bunch of money. I don't know how much. But a lot. My mom convinced my dad to move out here so I could be an actress. 'So I could follow my dreams,' she said. But we all know it's her dream."

"Your relationship with your mother seems . . . complicated."

"There was one night, back in Ohio, when I overheard them talking about moving here. It was, like, right after my grandpa died. My mom didn't waste any time. She told my dad, 'Beatrice's looks are wasted on this town. She could make us a lot of money, but not here.'" She looks out the window, tugging at a lock of her hair. "She said, 'If we stay here, she'll get knocked up by the time she's seventeen. She'll be fat and divorced before she's old enough to buy a goddamn beer.' I'll never forget that."

"That's . . . dark."

"That's my mom." She shrugs, sighing deeply. "The only thing I ever wanted was a real mom. I know I'm young, but I'm old enough to know what moms are supposed to be like. I used to go to friends' houses and wish I could trade places with them. I was always especially interested in the ugly girls. I wanted to see how their moms treated them. I would go over to their houses and expect their moms to be mean and angry because they were ugly, but they weren't. They were so nice. They loved those girls so much." She pauses. "I don't really go over to friends' houses anymore."

"Do you honestly think your mom only loves you because you're . . ." I falter, coughing awkwardly and clearing my throat. "Um, because you're pretty?"

"I don't think 'love' is the right word for what my mom feels about me. But, yeah. If I wasn't pretty, things would be a lot different. They'd be worse."

"You don't . . . know that," I say feebly.

"Yeah. I do. She counts my calories. I mean, like, for fuck's sake."

"You have to be careful about that kind of thing. It can lead you to . . . to some bad places."

She glares at me, full of hostility. "No shit. Great observation, detective. What would you know about it, anyway?"

I want to shrink into my seat. "Nothing," I say. "I don't know anything about it. I'm . . . sorry."

Sighing, Beatrice shakes her head and says, "No, I'm sorry. It's just kind of a delicate subject."

"I get it," I say, and I do. My stomach grumbles, and I can only hope she doesn't hear it.

"Where are you from?" Beatrice asks, clearly as eager as I am to change the topic.

"Bishop," I tell her. "It's a shitty little town about four hours north of here. Everyone there is ugly and drives pickup trucks. They eat at the same diner and drink at the same bar and go to the same church. I couldn't get out of there fast enough."

"Do you have family up there?"

I wince, and the side of my mouth twitches to the side a little. "Just my mom," I say. "We don't . . . talk much. My brothers are in New York, and I don't really talk to them, either. My dad's been dead for a while."

"Well, that explains a lot."

"What explains a lot?" I ask, glancing uncertainly at her. "And what does it . . . explain?"

"Your uncle is, like, some sort of fucked-up fill-in for your dad." She shrugs. "I mean, it makes sense. You had a void to fill, so you filled it."

I think of Beatrice's mother saying to her husband, *Have you considered, perhaps, that you're subconsciously trying to get closer to filling a surrogate void because you can't fill the one that's between your daughter's legs?* I shudder and push the thought away. "Don't try to figure me out," I say. "It's not worth it."

TEN
INAPPROPRIATE TEXTS

A few nights after the party, I'm lying on my futon, hoping I'll fall asleep before the yellow woman comes, when my phone vibrates. I pick it up and unlock it, and there's a text from a number with a 440 area code that says, *hey.*

I sit up and text back, *Who is this?*

The reply is almost instantaneous: *beatrice*, it says. She follows with, *do u ever get scared??*

I glance at the darkness seeping from my closet. *How did you get my number?* I type back.

i took it from my moms phone.

You shouldn't be texting me. It's inappropriate.

answer the question.

I sigh, ruffling my hair. The floorboards in my closet creak, and I can see the silhouette of the yellow woman, but she stays put for the time being. I reply back, *Scared of what?*

the cancer. r u scared it will come back?

Frowning, I type, *It's almost midnight. Why are you even awake?*

stop changing the subject.

The floorboards creak again. I can see the glow of the yellow woman's eyes, can smell the stale tobacco scent of her wrinkly flesh. I answer, *Sometimes. But I have a plan. If it comes back, I know exactly what I'm going to do.*

which is??

I take a moment to contemplate my situation. I'm sitting in bed, texting a fourteen-year-old girl about some Pretty Deep Shit that's none of her business. I don't like how it makes me feel. *Go back to sleep*, I text.

A minute passes. Two minutes. I should turn my phone off and go to sleep, myself, but I don't. I wait for her reply, hating the way my heart palpitates in the anticipatory moments before it comes.

i can't sleep. i keep thinking about ur cancer and it makes me really sad. ur so young.

It's not that sad. Lots of people get cancer. Lots of them are young.

so what's ur plan?

Sighing again, I get up and turn on the lights. The yellow woman hisses and recedes farther back into the closet. The light won't keep her from coming out, but it'll delay her a bit. I unscrew my smoke detector, light a cigarette, and type, *I have some money saved. Not a ton, but* enough. *If the cancer comes back, I'll take it out of the bank and fly to the Caribbean and spend my last days dying alone in the sun.* I hit "Send," and then type, *If my money runs out before the cancer kills me, I'll kill myself.* I deliberate for a moment before sending it.

It's almost a full five minutes before she replies. *that's awful*, she texts. *why wouldn't u fight it?*

I'm done fighting. I did plenty of fighting. I don't have any fight left in me.

but there r people who care about u.

Not really. I'm estranged from most of my family and I don't have a lot of friends. I flash on Judy. She'd miss me, but she'd get over it. I reconciled that piece of the equation a long time ago.

Six minutes passes before she replies, *i care about u.*

I stare at the screen. I'd be lying if I said I didn't feel a brief jolt of dopamine at those four words, but I quickly recognize it for what it is. I'm a sad, lonely man in a sad, lonely city. I can't remember the last time someone said they cared about me. I would have had the same absurd reaction if the words had been inside a fucking fortune cookie.

That's what I tell myself, anyway, and I can almost believe it. The yellow woman chuckles hideously from the darkness.

You don't even know me, I text back.

i know u well enough to care.

You're a child.

don't even start with that shit. Eye-rolling emoji.

Go to sleep.

when will i see u again?

I'll be in touch with your mom. Go to sleep.

fine. goodnight. And then, *i hope the cancer doesn't come back.* Heart emoji.

Me too. No emoji. I lay the phone facedown beside me, put out my cigarette, and screw the smoke detector back in. Almost as soon as I shut off the lights, the yellow woman crawls out on her hands and knees.

ELEVEN
PLAYING GOD

SOMETIMES, I hurt people weaker than I am.

Inflicting suffering upon the weak is the closest a man can get to playing God.

The first time I deliberately hurt another human being—*really* hurt him—was the day after I'd been diagnosed. I was walking around Hollywood late at night. Never a good idea, especially if you're alone, as I was, but I was feeling reckless. Unhinged. I was twenty-three years old, and my life was unraveling at the seams. I'd come to Los Angeles to become a person of power and influence. Instead, I was power*less*, afflicted with cancer and relying on my rich uncle to pay my medical bills. My only probable prospects for the future were disease and death.

I don't even remember what street I'd been on when the homeless kid approached me, but it had been dark and quiet and still. It was late, and it wasn't a main thoroughfare, so there hadn't been any traffic or pedestrians. Raving, slavering, yellow-eyed and bone-thin, the boy had emerged from one of the innumerable tents and started shuffling straight for me. His frail arms pinwheeled. The stench of shit rose from his tattered clothes as he drew closer. I detected the words "spare change" intermingled with the nonsensical babble coming from his mostly toothless mouth.

He was probably harmless. I don't think he'd been any older than fifteen, but it's hard to tell with them. No matter his age, though, I could have quickened my pace and turned down the next street. Usually, when they realize you're not going to acknowledge their existence, they give up. I could have ignored him, and that would have been that.

But that's not what I did.

I stopped walking and turned to face him. His grime-encrusted face brightened, and he loped toward me with a feeble gait, braying and hooting madly. When he was close enough, I punched him in the face. He flew backward off his heels and landed in a sitting position, looking up at me, whimpering like a dog as he put his hands to his bleeding nose. I stared down at him, breathing heavily, hating him. How dare he come to *me*, mumbling unintelligible entreaties for mercy, when God or the universe or whatever refused to grant me any such kindness?

As the kid started to crawl back toward his tent, I looked around and ascertained there was still no one in the immediate vicinity. I spotted a broken metal rod lying nearby amid scraps of garbage. I picked it up and approached the boy. He had nearly reached his tent when I grabbed his ankle and hauled him backward, disgusted by the slimy feel of his skin.

He was light, and dragging him was easy. When he was a safe distance away from safety, I released my grip and lorded over him, caressing my makeshift weapon. He rolled onto his back and began whimpering some more. I hit him in the jaw with the rod, surely dislodging whatever teeth remained there. He cried out, blood bubbling onto his chin. I hit him a couple of times in the ribs. I shattered both of his kneecaps. I went to work on his bare feet, bludgeoning them until they were useless, misshapen slabs of flesh. I remember how his left foot split open down the middle. It's not something you forget.

I don't know how long I kept beating him. I mainly avoided his head, because I didn't want to kill him. Not out of any last-ditch act of clemency; I just wanted to be sure he lived long enough to suffer. I wanted the whole world to feel my pain, and since I didn't have the means to make that happen, the homeless kid had to stand in for the rest of them.

Looking down at the kid, bloodied and broken, I was struck by an inexplicable image of a young boy in a gore-spattered room, naked and shivering, standing over another boy who appeared to be dead. Shaken and bewildered, I shoved the image away and dropped the rod, now sticky with blood and hair. I looked one last time at the kid before walking away.

I didn't feel any better.

I didn't feel any worse.

TWELVE

THINGS YOU'RE SUPPOSED TO SAY

I wake shivering from forgotten dreams, tangled in sheets drenched in cool sweat. The gray morning light slinking through the blinds is cold on my skin.

I sit straight up, my muscles seizing and my heart plunking into my stomach like a heavy rock dropped into a pond. The hollow splash is nearly audible.

"No," I say aloud, hating the terrified whimper in my voice. "No, no, please no." I put a hand to the scar on my neck, momentarily certain I'll feel the beginnings of a foreign lump. There's nothing there, but, of course, there wouldn't be. The first time around—and I shudder at that thought, at the implication it wasn't the *last* time—the night sweats had preceded the tumor's appearance by a couple of years.

It won't be so slow this time.

The voice comes from within, but it has the sandpapery timbre of the yellow woman's throaty growl. I get up and turn on the lights, and in the periphery of my vision I see a blur of movement as something—as *she*—scampers into the darkness of my closet.

"Stay there," I whisper. "I can't deal with you right now."

There's a rustling from the other side of the partially ajar closet door, but for now she remains confined.

Only for now, though.

Only for now.

· · ·

Judy Kaplan opens the front door of her Malibu mansion, looking like her new self. I always expect Judy Coover to appear, her gothic punk affectations restored, but she never does. When she'd married the nice, rich Jewish boy, she'd abandoned all that in favor of a chic, Malibu housewife aesthetic. Lots of pearls and diamonds, and designer dresses flirting with the line between modest and slutty. It probably happened before the marriage, I'm sure; the transformation had most likely started to take effect not long after she'd been introduced to him and his music industry money, but we hadn't been talking at that point.

"You shouldn't be here," Judy says. "I told you. I keep telling you. You have to stop coming here unannounced. You shouldn't be coming here at all."

I raise my eyebrow at her, glancing back at the driveway. "I don't see Isaac's car," I say. I look over her shoulder into the clean, well-lighted, open space of the huge house. "Is he here?"

She bites her lip and fidgets with her wedding ring. "No. He took Grayden to Disneyland."

"Isn't he kind of old for Disneyland?"

"He's three, actually."

"I meant Isaac. Actually."

Her mouth twitches. I can't tell if it's the faltered beginning of an in-spite-of-herself smile or a disapproving frown. "Ty," she says. "Don't."

"Why aren't you with them?"

"It isn't like that. It's not a big deal."

I lower my gaze. The welcome mat is askew. I right it with the toe of my shoe. "Look," I say, running my hand through my hair. "Can I come in?"

"We have to stop doing this."

"Agreed. One hundred percent. I just want to talk."

"A phone call would have sufficed."

"Would you have answered?"

She bites her lip again and sighs. She moves out of the doorway.

Judy leads me out back to the pool deck overlooking the ocean and sits at a triangular glass table. I sit across from her. She calls out something in Spanish to a shirtless teenage boy who's cleaning the pool, and he stops what he's doing and goes inside. A salt-smelling sea breeze teases Judy's hair, which isn't as long as it had been in college. Her wild curls are flat-ironed straight. "You look thin," she says, crossing her tan legs. "Still not eating?"

I take my cigarettes out of my shirt pocket and light one. She slides a gold ashtray toward me from the center of the table. "I eat when it's necessary," I say, turning my head to blow smoke toward the pool. It floats over the still water until another breeze scatters its wispy plumes.

"Mm. You've always had a weird idea of what's 'necessary.' Did you ever see that therapist?"

"I don't need a therapist."

She purses her lips. "You know, I have this friend. He's a psychiatrist. I told him about you. I didn't use your name, of course. Relax. But I told him about you, and you know what he said? He said he's never encountered a case of a male eating disorder that wasn't in some way related to sexual trauma."

"Christ, Judy. Not that shit again."

The boy reappears with two flutes of pink champagne, which he sets before us on the table. Judy thanks him in Spanish, and he goes back inside.

"Are we celebrating something?" I ask, tapping ash into the ashtray. There are about ninety-five calories in a glass of champagne. All I've eaten today is a couple pieces of lettuce, so I can afford it.

Judy shrugs. "I don't know," she says. "Saturday afternoon?" She takes a sip, closes her eyes, and smiles mirthfully. "Honestly, I just love this stuff. Can't get enough of it. Anyway. Back to your sexual trauma."

"We've been over this. I'm pretty sure I'd know if someone had fucking diddled me when I was a kid. And really, stop saying 'trauma.' It's a ridiculous word."

"What's ridiculous about it?"

"I don't know, it's . . . the connotations, I guess. It's so . . . earnest. Whatever. There's nothing there. Besides, my eating habits are totally under control. I didn't come here to talk about that."

"Then what did you come here to talk about?"

I drag from my cigarette, looking out at the ocean rolling restlessly beneath the heavy gray clouds. Rubbing my scar, I take one deep breath, then another. "I think it's back," I say. I look at Judy. Her eyes soften, turning from hard sapphires to shimmering tide pools. For the millionth time, I wish I could have loved her.

"What makes you think that?" she asks.

"Nothing concrete. Just a feeling." I pause, hit the cigarette. "But the night sweats started again."

"That's kind of concrete."

"Not necessarily."

"It's more than a feeling. I mean, what *feeling* are you even talking about?"

"It's the same feeling I had when the biopsy results came back as 'suspicious.' That was when I knew. They told me there was still a high probability it was benign, but I knew." I crush out my cigarette and take a long pull from the champagne. "I know now. It's back."

It looks for a second like her eyes have welled up with tears, but she blinks and they're gone so fast it could have been my imagination. She reaches across the table and clasps my hand. Her grip is warm, and it feels like home. "Jesus, Ty. You don't *know*, okay? You're a very paranoid person. That's probably all it is. But, still . . . you should call your oncologist. Tell her about the night sweats."

"I have a routine checkup in September. The annual PET scan, and all that. I'll mention it then."

"That's not soon enough. If it *is* back, you should get yourself checked out as soon as possible."

I shake my head and look into the bubbling depths of the champagne. "I have a lot going on right now. I'm in the middle of helping my uncle with this project—"

"The pizza thing?"

"It's about more than pizza."

"Knowing your uncle, it's probably super shady."

"It's not that shady."

"Whatever it is, it's not that *important*. Your *health* is important. Fuck Arthur. Take care of *you*." She squeezes my hand when she emphasizes the last word. "I mean, God, what did you expect me to say? Did you think you could come here and tell me this and I'd be all, 'Oh, most definitely, prioritize some shitty commercial for your uncle's money laundering front, and to hell with your health'?"

"To tell you the truth, I didn't think that far ahead. I had to talk to someone. I had to say it out loud. You were the first person I thought of." I bite my lip, lowering my gaze. "You were the only person I thought of."

The little smile she gives me is full of sadness. "You're not allowed to die, Tyler Seward. I want you around."

I snort. "What does it matter to you?" I say, crueler than I'd intended. Dialing back my tone, I add, "You're the one who keeps telling me to stop coming here."

She nods and downs the rest of her drink. "Yes. Well. I suppose I've gotten so used to saying the things I'm supposed to, that sometimes I say them to the wrong people." She stands and holds out her hand. "Come on. Let's go inside."

I look up at her. "I wasn't looking for a pity fuck, you know."

"I know. But it seems you've found one anyway. Besides, it's not *just* pity." She winks.

I take her hand.

• • •

Judy finally gives up and gets out of bed. I'm full of shame as I look at my flaccid dick—wet with her saliva but not her vaginal fluid—as Judy pulls on her panties and re-clasps her bra. I watch her as she goes to the mirror on the bureau and smooths her hair back into place. She looks over her shoulder at me and says, "Would it have helped if I'd asked my maid for her feather duster?"

I scowl. It's been a long time since she's mentioned that incident. "Is that why we didn't work out?" I ask. "Because of the feather duster?"

Judy comes over to sit on the edge of the bed, passing her hand through my hair. "No, Ty, that's not why we didn't work out. We didn't work out because you're a bit of a narcissist, and you're fundamentally incapable of relating to other human beings." She uses her thumb to brush an eyelash off my face. "You also cheated on me. There is *that*." She kisses my cheek, my lips. "But the feather duster thing *was* weird, honestly. It's something you should bring up if you ever go see that therapist."

"I'm not going to see the therapist."

She shrugs and looks at my cock, giving it a little flick. "You've never had this problem before," she says. "Literally, never."

"That's not true. There was that time after the premiere of one of Arthur's movies, when I got super drunk and did all that coke."

"No, even then, I eventually got you there. It just took a while. This was way different."

"Well, I'm sorry."

"Oh, God, don't be. You'd be surprised at how low Isaac's batting average is. It's a wonder Grayden was ever conceived."

"I don't think I'd be that surprised."

She smacks my arm. "He's a good husband. He's reliable and he takes care of me and Grayden."

"If he took care of you, you wouldn't have any use for me."

"It's more complicated than that. And what we just did—scratch that, what *I* just did, or *tried* to do—it's not exactly my idea of being taken care of, so you're not in a position to be smug. I'm going to have to get out my Jack Rabbit when you leave so I can finish what you clearly never should have started."

"You started it," I point out. "Will you at least think of me?"

She grins and shakes her head. "Sorry, I'm actually planning to pic-ture–" She names a popular movie star. I bite the inside of my cheek. I doubt she'd fantasize about him if she knew he likes to skull-fuck dead pre-teen boys.

Judy must detect something in my face because she asks, "What's wrong? Have you met him?"

I think about the way the movie star always insists upon cutting out the pre-teen boys' tongues so he can take them home with him, and I say, "Um, no, I don't think so. No. I haven't met him."

THIRTEEN

THE PRETENDER

Y OU want me to . . . take my clothes off?" Beatrice says, looking uneasily at Arthur, at the sound guys, at the lighting guys, at the camera crew, at me. I can only hold her gaze for a moment before I have to look away. All the crew members are trying to appear busy, setting up lights and equipment and pointedly not looking in Beatrice's direction.

We're in a private soundstage on Arthur's compound. We spent most of the day shooting the TV spot on location at the pizza parlor, but what we're about to shoot isn't going to end up on television. This is something separate.

"Dolly, baby," says Arthur, hunkering down on one knee and touching Beatrice's face. "This is *showbiz*. You're a part of something special, yeah? What we're about to shoot, only the richest and most powerful players in Hollywood are going to see. They're going to see *you*, and they're going to *want* you. And if *they* want you, *everyone* will want you."

"But . . . if I'm, like, *naked* . . . then it's porn. It's child porn, right? We're making child porn?"

There's a flicker of a grimace on Arthur's face, but he recovers with a flashy smile. "No, Dolly, sweetheart, this is *art.*"

Someone wheels in a catering cart loaded with pizza ingredients.

"It's going to be very tasteful," Arthur assures Beatrice. "Think, I don't know, Andy Warhol, or something."

Beatrice eyes the catering cart and hugs her shoulders, shivering.

"I know it's chilly in here," says Arthur, "but once you're under the lights you'll be, ah, quite warm. I promise." He stands, grinning at Beatrice. "You know you're getting paid extra for this, right? Off the books. Ty, you told her, yeah?"

"I haven't told her anything." He told me not to tell her anything.

"Forgive my nephew," Arthur says, shooting daggers at me. "He's forgetful. Two thousand dollars, straight under the table. You know what under the table means, don't you?"

I can see Beatrice trying to decide if a fourteen-year-old should know something like that. Finally, she shrugs and nods.

"Good, I knew it, you're a bright girl. Now, come on, let's get those clothes off, yeah? We're going out to celebrate once we're done here, so the sooner we get going, the sooner we can get gone."

• • •

I don't want to watch Beatrice undress, but Arthur makes me.

74

She stares at me the whole time. Her movements are hurried but somehow consciously sensuous. First, she kicks off her heels. She slides down her cutoff denim shorts. She peels off her tank top. She stands there in her bra and panties and looks at me for a moment before unclasping the bra and stepping out of her underwear.

The whole time, she's staring at me.

I don't know what that means.

• • •

Lying beneath the lights, covered in pizza sauce, and with pepperonis glued over her nipples, Beatrice does whatever Arthur tells her to do. She rolls around in anchovies and olives. She pleasures herself—or pretends to—with a frozen sausage. Somebody squeezes pepper juice into her eyes. A teenage boy masturbates into a hunk of raw dough someone has fashioned to look like a crude penis, which Arthur tells Beatrice to eat. I think about all the calories in that dough, and I feel sad for her. Semen only has between five and twenty-five calories per ejaculation, but the dough is another story.

This goes on for about an hour and a half, with the cameraman capturing every last minute of it, never cutting. Arthur will edit it into a three-minute teaser reel to be discreetly distributed to "investors," and the scraps will get filed away for his personal use.

This isn't even the worst video of its kind Arthur has done. At least there weren't any animals this time. There was one with pit bulls that doesn't bear mentioning. The girl—she'd been eleven—killed herself a few weeks later. Arthur didn't attend the memorial. I did.

When it's over, Arthur dismisses everyone but me and Beatrice, and I have to watch as he fucks her on the bed of pizza slop. He lasts much longer than he did the first time. He cycles through a variety of positions, and Beatrice goes along with all of it. At the end, after he's ejaculated onto her topping-strewn face, he even goes down on her in a rare display of—what? Generosity? Is that even right? Beatrice seems to enjoy this—or, at least, she makes a convincing show of enjoying it. I sort of feel something as she begins gasping—softly, at first, and then developing into back-arching, toe-curling cries of apparent ecstasy—but I can't figure out what it is. Usually, witnessing this type of thing makes me feel a vague sense of revulsion, but this time it's something else. Something I can't place. I prefer the revulsion.

When Beatrice's orgasm—or faux orgasm, whatever it is—reaches its completion, leaving her collapsed and panting amid the mess, Arthur gets up and tells me to take her to the guest house so she can shower. "I'll meet you two at Guide Bar in an hour," he says, toweling pizza toppings off his person and looking pleased with himself. "I've got the whole place reserved, so it'll just be us and some of the crew." With a wink, he adds, "And my date." He starts to leave, but then, seemingly forgetting something, he holds up his finger and stops. He reaches into the pocket of his discarded jeans and takes out a baggie of coke, which he hands to me and says, "Don't hog it all to yourself. Let her have a taste. But not too much, yeah? She's quite young, remember."

• • •

While Beatrice is showering in the master bathroom of the guest house, I do some of the coke before sitting on the bed to smoke a cigarette. Arthur never comes in the guest house, so he lets people smoke in here. I watch the hazy blue plumes rising to the ceiling so I don't have to look at myself in the mirror on the closet door across from me.

As I sit there listening to the sounds of the shower coming from the bathroom, I wonder what Beatrice might be thinking as she stands beneath the water. I'm not great at taking other people's thoughts and feelings into consideration—it was one of Judy's biggest hang-ups with me when we were together—but I'm genuinely curious. How does a person—especially one her age—bounce back from what Arthur just put her through? Remembering the pit bulls and the eleven-year-old girl, I wonder for a moment if it's possible to bounce back at all, but I quickly dismiss the notion. That had been something else altogether. Still, I can't imagine Beatrice's experience would be an easy one to move past. Maybe it'll be enough to disillusion her from the entertainment industry and she'll quit acting, her mother's aspirations be damned. For some reason I can't put my finger on, I hope this is the case.

I hear the water shut off and, after a few moments, the sound of the hair dryer. I crush out my cigarette and do some more of the coke. It's better than the coke that had been served at the party last week. Not as cut. I wonder where Arthur gets it from, and for how much. This gets me stewing in resentment; whenever I buy coke, it's shit. I should have access to whatever channels Arthur does. I shouldn't be forced to snort Sweet 'N' Low simply because I'm not a "player." More than that, I should *be* a player. I was never suited for the life of a peasant. By design, I should be at Arthur's level, or higher. I could certainly come up with better uses for my money than making underage girls roll around in fucking pizza ingredients.

Beatrice emerges from the bathroom amid a cloud of steam, like a pop star making an extravagant stage entrance. She's wrapped in a towel, and she asks where her clothes are. I point to the armchair in the corner of the bedroom, where I've laid her folded garments. Instead of collecting them, she looks at me strangely for a moment, and then she drops the towel. I look away and light another cigarette, telling myself the tremors in my hands are from the coke, or maybe because the only thing I've eaten today is a baby carrot and half a granola bar.

"What's wrong?" Beatrice asks, her voice somewhat barbed, like she's baiting me. "You've seen me naked twice now. Like, *really* naked. *All* the naked. Why are you suddenly ashamed?"

"I didn't want to see. Arthur—"

"Right, right, he *made* you. But ... did he?" From the corner of my eye, I see the hazy silhouette of her figure take a step toward me. Then another. "If you want to look, why not admit it? Why do you have to hide what you want behind what Arthur wants?"

"I don't want to look."

"Really? Why not? I know what I look like. I know I definitely don't look like a kid. I have a woman's body. You like women, don't you? Come on. I'm giving you a free pass to look without having to see your uncle sweating on top of me or behind me, or whatever." She pauses, clucking her tongue. "Or, like, is that a thing for you? Do you get something out of seeing him fuck me? Is it like that with all the girls?"

"No. Jesus. Stop." I hit my cigarette.

"You're shaking. Is it because you want to touch me? Do you want to grab me and throw me on the bed and–" her voice hitches "–shove your cock inside me?"

"For fuck's sake, *no*," I say, standing and facing her. I'd only been intending to shoot a contemptuous glare her way and re-avert my eyes, but then I see the fat tears rolling down her face. "You're crying," I say, tensing. I'm not good at dealing with crying women. "Why are you crying. You . . . don't have to–"

She cuts me off by closing the distance between us and throwing her arms around me, sobbing into my chest. I have no idea how to react. Do I return the embrace? Do I push her off me? Do I just stand here and let her cry? I decide the final option is the safest one, so I stand there awkwardly with her naked body pressed against me. I think of maggot-chewed corpses, of festering sores, of gangrenous lesions and pus-oozing wounds, of shitting cats and massive Australian spiders and the hard calluses that form on your heel and–

"I wish you'd *stop*," she says, finally pulling away. I let out a breath. She puts her hand to her forehead and closes her eyes.

"Stop . . . what?"

"Pretending like you're not what you are." She opens her eyes and stares at me with a sadness so profound I want to curl into a ball, just to escape it. "That's why you hide behind your uncle. You're too afraid to look at yourself."

I glance at my reflection in the mirror on the closet door, but all I see is a thin man who isn't thin enough.

Beatrice says, "I just wish you'd stop pretending."

"I'm not pretending," I say to the mirror.

"I don't think you even know you're doing it. But you are. It's weird that you hate actors so much, because you're the best one I've ever seen. You're so good you don't even know you're acting. You don't see that you're not what you pretend to be."

"Who am I then?" I ask the mirror.

"I don't know. I can't figure it out." She sniffles. "But you're not what you pretend to be."

I look at her, keeping my eyes level with hers. "I don't . . . know what that means. And I don't know why you're . . . sad about it. I don't know why you're . . . crying."

"It confuses me," she says, wiping her left eye with the heel of her hand and the right eye with the back of it. "It's hard to explain. It doesn't . . . it doesn't fit. You don't fit with everything else. I want to know which things are bad and which things are good. I want it to be easy."

"Nothing is . . . easy," is the only thing I can think of to say.

"I want it to be," she says in her child's voice, but this time I know she isn't acting.

FOURTEEN

SOUL BARGAINING

GUIDE BAR is on Franklin, between Birds and La Poubelle, but I can't find parking. I spend fifteen minutes driving in relative circles, and I'm on the verge of screaming when at last a space opens up on Tamarind. I pull into it right as a BMW pulls out, much to the chagrin of the driver of an approaching Mercedes. After I take the key out of the ignition, I sit in silence for a few moments, waiting for my anger-accelerated heartbeat to return to normal.

"Ty?" Beatrice says. "Are you okay?"

I take a deep breath, trying to enjoy the gigantic flood of relief that comes with finding a decent parking space. "I'm fine," I say. "I just hate this town sometimes."

"Why do you live here, then?"

I sigh, watching a pretty redhead standing at the Daily Planet's newsstand flip through an issue of *Variety*. A chihuahua waits patiently for her, affixed to a leash wrapped around her tan, slender wrist. "I have to live here," I explain. "I have aspirations. Things I can only accomplish if I'm here."

"Things like directing a version of *Romeo and Juliet* that no one is going to see?"

I throw her a look, one that I guess says something like, *Go fuck yourself.* "It's bigger than that," I say, lighting a cigarette. "There's . . . a lot more to it."

I can feel her studying me, measuring her words. "You should be careful," she says. "Someone told me once that you can lose your soul to this town if you get too, like, caught up in it."

"If LA wants my soul," I say, "it can have it. It just has to give me something in return."

"It's just a city, Ty. It's just a place. It's not like it's alive."

"It *is* alive. You don't see it yet, but if you stay here long enough, you will. Living here is like . . . It's like having a horrible girlfriend who's nice to look at, but she dodges your calls and sleeps with your friends. I mean, she doesn't just sleep with them, she fucking bangs them right in front of you. She ties you down and makes you watch as she fulfills their wildest fantasies, and when she's done and you think it's finally your turn, she sends you home because she's got a fucking headache. And you keep subjecting yourself to it, night after night, hanging on to the hope that she'll one day see you for what you are, and that she'll realize no one will ever love her like you do."

Beatrice takes the cigarette from me and hits it. She hands it back and says, holding the smoke in her lungs, "You just said you hate her."

She releases the smoke and amends, "I mean, *it*. Criminy, now you've got me doing it."

"It's complicated. It's a love/hate thing. Ask your parents, I have a feeling they'd know what I'm talking about."

Beatrice's face falls and she looks at her lap. She doesn't say anything for a while, and I'm starting to wonder if I've gone too far when she says, "No. My parents just hate each other."

Outside, the redhead has put the *Variety* back on the stand and is now lighting a joint and walking up Tamarind. She glances at me as she passes my car. I look away.

Raising her head, Beatrice says, "I don't have a fake ID, or anything. Is that going to be a problem at this bar we're going to?"

"No," I tell her. "Arthur spends so much money there he practically owns the place."

"Good."

"Just . . . don't drink too much. I still have to take you home, remember."

With narrowed eyes and a cruel, mirthless smile, she says, "Your uncle made me debase myself in front of strangers before fucking me on a bed of pizza toppings. I'll drink as much as I goddamn want to."

• • •

Beatrice holds fast to her assertion; as soon as we're inside the bar, she starts drinking. She begins by chugging a cosmopolitan, then a second one. After that, two of the crew members start buying her shots. I sit a few stools away, watching helplessly, sipping my rum and Diet Coke and trying to focus on the comforting fact it only has sixty-four calories.

Arthur arrives not too long after we do, sporting a stunning blonde on his arm who has the coldest, meanest face I've ever seen on an attractive woman. She looks like she's maybe a few years younger than I am, but you can never tell with girls in this city. Arthur introduces her to me as Ianthe, distractedly explains she's about to graduate from UCLA with a double major in Biology and Chemistry, and then he abandons her to go get stoned in a booth with some of the crewmembers. I look anxiously over at Beatrice, who's lining up another shot of something I can only hope—but honestly doubt—has a relatively reasonable alcohol by volume.

"Can I . . . get you a drink?" I say feebly to Ianthe.

She fixes her icy stare on me and shrugs. "Yeah, whatever," she sighs. "I'll have a Belvedere on the rocks."

I call over the bartender—a short brunette whom Arthur is fond of, and whom he usually insists be called in to work whenever he reserves the place—and order the drink. I watch her make it, stewing with silent dread at the prospect of having to engage in conversation with the severe, hostile woman standing beside me. I hand her the vodka and say, "So, um, how did you and Arthur . . . meet?" A risky question, but the only one I can think of at the moment.

Ianthe shrugs again, sipping her drink through the swizzle stick. "A friend of mine used to do some work for him."

"Oh . . . really? What's . . . her name?"

"Mara," she says, not bothering to give a last name, but it doesn't ring a bell so it doesn't matter. "You wouldn't know her. It was a long time ago. We were in high school." She stirs the ice around. "She's dead now."

"I'm . . . sorry."

"It was a long time ago," she repeats. "Anyway, I was at one of Arthur's parties last week and he invited me to this . . . whatever this is." She looks around, scowling. "I'm not sure why I agreed."

Because he's rich. Because he's powerful. And because no matter how repulsive of a person he is, and no matter what sort of sick shit he made your friend do back in the day, you're still going to fuck him tonight.

"The playlist . . . isn't bad," I offer, even though I have no idea what's playing on the sound system right now.

"I think it blows," says Ianthe.

"Right. Um. Speaking of which, I, ah, have some. I was about to—"

"No, thank you," she says abruptly, her face darkening. "I don't do drugs."

"That's not something you hear often in this city."

"Whatever. I had a bad experience with them." She stirs the ice in her drink. "People got hurt. People died."

"Sounds like they weren't doing it right."

Ianthe says nothing, just glares at me.

I clear my throat. "Right, well. I'll . . . be back."

"Take your time. Please."

I start for the bathroom, relieved I won't have to share the coke, but then Beatrice breaks away from her entourage and stops me, grabbing my arm. "Are you going to . . . *get high*?" she slurs, whispering the last two words. Her face is slack, her eyes distant. She's swaying on her feet. The smell of alcohol on her breath is noxious.

"Yes," I say, "I'm going to *get high*." I'd been intending to forbid her from partaking, but seeing her as drunk as she is gives me second thoughts; it might, actually, sober her up a bit. "Come on," I say, making no attempt to mask my reluctance.

The restroom is one of those single-service unisex deals—or bi-gender or all-gender or whatever you want to call it—so we have it to ourselves. Once inside, I flick the lock on the heavy wooden door and take the coke out, carefully pouring some of it on the tip of my car key. I do a bump, pour some more out for a second bump, and offer the third bump to Beatrice. She bends over and snorts it. Her head whips back and she stumbles, pressing her palm against the wall for support. "*Whoa*," she breathes. "That feels *amazing*. Like, *way* more amazing than last time."

"I know. It's from Arthur's personal stash, so it's better quality."

She laughs, probably because she's drunk and high since I don't know what about that statement was funny. "Give me more," she says, reaching for the baggie.

I stuff the coke back in my pocket and tell her no, holding my finger up to her like she's a disobedient child. "You seriously have to cool it,"

I say. "You are way too fucked up."

"I'm not fucked up *enough*," she says, her wired eyes boring into mine. At least her speech is a little clearer. "I did the work, now it's time for me to play."

"You're still a kid."

Frowning, Beatrice says, "Uh-uh. No *way*. You don't get to say that. I'm either a kid or I'm not—you don't get to choose when to treat me like a kid and when to treat me like a grownup based on when it's convenient. What I had to do today was not something that kids have to do."

I think about pointing out that Arthur made her do it *because* she's a kid, but that probably wouldn't serve any purpose, so I don't say anything.

"Who was that girl you were talking to?" Beatrice asks, and I'm as surprised by the abrupt change of subject as I am by the intense manner in which she's looking at me.

"Arthur's date," I answer. Then, spurred by the coke or maybe by something else I can't confront, I add, "Why? Are you jealous?"

"Of him, or of you?"

I think about it. "Both. Either. I don't know." I shrug.

"Should I be?"

"Of me, or of Arthur?"

"Both. Either." She shrugs. Her smile is devious. "I don't know."

"Very funny. Listen, we should go back."

"Are you afraid of what the others will think if we're in here too long?"

"I don't care what anyone thinks. About anything."

Beatrice tilts her head to the side and kind of squints at me, biting her lip. "You say that. You *act* like that. But I think you care very much what other people think."

"We should . . . go back," is all I'm able to say.

Huffing dramatically, she flips her hair and says, "Fine. But you better tell me if you come back in here to do more, because *I* want more."

"I will," I lie. "A little later."

• • •

Returning to the bar, I order another rum and Diet, ruminating on how I should have hung back in the bathroom and done the rest of the coke. I'm not nearly high enough, and this whole thing is such a drag. I glance at Beatrice, who's dancing by herself on the dance floor to a pop song I don't recognize, something bubblegummy and obnoxious that clashes with my dour mood. Beatrice's movements, to her credit, are in sync with the beat and, admittedly, provocative enough to make me kind of uncomfortable.

Ianthe has migrated away from the bar and is standing stiffly by the retro-style jukebox I'm pretty sure is just for show, getting talked at by a couple of camera guys who might as well be salivating. Next to me, a lighting guy is holding his phone out to a sound guy, showing him a picture of something I can't see from this angle.

"Yeah, no, I don't think so, man," Sound Guy is saying as he contemplates whatever image is on the screen. He scratches his jaw. "I think you're being paranoid. That's definitely the work of a coyote."

"*Dude*," says Lighting Guy, flustered. He looks at the phone and shakes his head. "You're fuckin' on one. Its head is cut *clean* off. Here, what about this?" He swipes the screen and shows it to Sound Guy.

Sound Guy leans forward, squinting hard at the screen. "No way, man. I'm sorry, I just don't buy that a person did that. I'm telling you. It was a coyote."

"There's a perfect *square* sliced out of its *stomach*."

"Dude," says Sound Guy, widening his eyes. "Coyotes are really smart. You don't even know. There was a whole thing on the Discovery Channel. Or maybe Animal Planet. You know, one of those sorts of deals."

Lighting Guy zooms in on the picture. "Its eyes are gouged out, man."

Shrugging, Sound Guy says, "Maybe a . . . skunk? Their paws are way tiny. A skunk could claw out a squirrel's eyes, no problem."

Lighting Guy shakes his head again and looks over at me. I have no desire to enter this conversation, so I pretend I'm invisible. Manifest your reality, and all that. It doesn't work. "Mr. Seward, sir," he says, "could you settle a dispute for us?"

I don't tell him I'd rather get ass-fucked by a chimpanzee. I don't tell him he is beneath me, their "dispute" is beneath me, this whole fucking scene is beneath me. I tell him, "Sure, what's up?" I'm gripping my drink so tightly I'm amazed the glass doesn't shatter. I wish it would.

Lighting Guy swipes back to the first picture and shows it to me. I grimace. "What exactly am I looking at here?" I say, rattling the ice in my drink.

"It's a cat. It . . . was a cat."

"I can see that." The cat in question is lying on its back with its legs spread-eagled and its tail pointing straight down. Its head has been removed and is situated between its hind legs, as if it's performing oral sex on itself. Lighting Guy swipes to the second picture, which is of a dead squirrel. The squirrel's legs are missing, and a rectangular hole has been cut into its abdomen. The organs appear to have been taken out. Its eyes are empty sockets.

"These were in my driveway," says Lighting Guy. "The cat was last week. The squirrel was this morning."

"Okay?" I draw the word out, wanting a cigarette or a cyanide capsule or absolutely anything to get me away from these morons.

"He thinks there's a psycho killer on the loose in his neighborhood," says Sound Guy, rolling his eyes. "This motherfucker lives in fucking *Atwater*."

"Well. Um. Atwater is . . . nice," is the only response I can come up with.

"You gotta admit, there's no *way* a coyote did that shit," says Lighting Guy.

I glance back at the picture. "I don't know a lot about . . . coyotes," I say. "I must have missed the thing on the Discovery Channel."

"Actually," says Sound Guy, "now that I think about it, it was definitely Animal Planet."

"I tried calling the police," says Lighting Guy, "but they were no help, as usual. They were all like, 'What do you want us to do about it?' And I was totally like, 'Uh, I don't know, maybe patrol my block at night so you can catch the wacko who's doing this?' But then I think the call dropped since I was at the Griffith Observatory meeting this girl—who didn't show *up*, for whatever it's worth—and you know how service is up there, and I thought about calling back but I decided not to in case the call *didn't* drop and they just hung up on me."

"They definitely hung up on you, dude," says Sound Guy somberly. "I get great service at the Observatory."

"Yeah, but I have Sprint," Lighting Guy points out.

"Mmm, fair play," says Sound Guy.

"I just would have thought," says Lighting Guy, "that the cops would care more about this type of thing, you know? Like, haven't they seen *Don't Fuck with Cats*? It's obviously a *person* who's doing this— *not* a goddamn coyote—and any person who can kill a cat is *for sure* going to start killing people eventually."

"Yeah, no, I don't fully buy that," says Sound Guy. "When I was a kid, I used to go to the junkyard and throw firecrackers at the strays and, I mean, I turned out pretty okay."

Lighting Guy thinks about this for a second. "No," he says, "I think that's different. Because you were a kid, and you grew out of it, right? Besides, I assume the cats died, like instantly?"

"Nah, not all of them."

"Still, that's kind of not the same thing as cutting off its head."

Sound Guy nods, mulling it over. "No, you're right. But where do we stand on the squirrel? Even if it *was* a person who did that shit to the squirrel—which I doubt—is he even dangerous? Because, like, it's a rodent, you know? It's not like it's cute or cuddly. It's basically a bushy-tailed rat."

"I think squirrels are cute," says Lighting Guy.

"But not cuddly," says Sound Guy.

"No," agrees Lighting Guy. "I guess not." He looks back at me, deadly serious. "Mr. Seward, what say you on squirrels?"

I blink, dazed, unable to impede the plummeting freefall in which my IQ is currently suspended. "Listen, guys," I say. "I just remembered I have to . . . make a phone call. I'll . . . be right back." I throw back the rest of my drink and set the glass on the bar before beelining for the door, my temples beginning to throb.

Before I'm able to make it out the door for my much-needed cigarette, Beatrice is suddenly in my way, blocking my path, dancing in place to a synthy cover of "Stayin' Alive." "Dance with me," she says.

"No."

"Come on, I'm the only one dancing. Please?" I can almost feel the gust of air when she bats her long eyelashes.

"I don't dance."

"I doubt that." She dances closer to me, mouthing the words to the song.

"It wouldn't be . . . appropriate," I say, feeling desperate, glancing over her at the door leading to my escape.

"But you want to. I saw you watching me."

"Everyone was watching you. You're making a fool of yourself." This isn't exactly true, but I'm a cornered animal. I guess this is how the cat had felt right before someone had cut its head off.

Beatrice isn't fazed by the insult. "Then come help me *not* make a fool of myself."

I rub the back of my neck, looking at the door again. I suddenly feel eyes on me—not Beatrice's. Arthur is watching me from his booth, his lips peeled back in a wolfish grin. The look in his eyes, the ghosts behind his smile, tell me everything he doesn't need to say. I sigh. Beatrice senses my capitulation and takes my hand, leading me onto the dance floor.

I hadn't been lying when I'd said I don't dance; I don't, but I can. I'm no Michael Jackson, but I'm competent enough, which Beatrice soon realizes with delight. "Hey, you're pretty good," she says, allowing me to twirl her. "Did someone teach you?"

"Yes," I say, thinking of Judy and wondering what she'd have to say if she knew her tutelage was being used with a precocious fourteen-year-old. I pull Beatrice to me and dip her. Arthur is still watching me—I can feel it the same way you can feel a spider crawling on the back of your neck—but I won't look at him.

"Well, you're full of surprises."

"Not really. I think this is the only surprise I have in me."

"How about you let *me* be the judge of that?" She spins so her back is pressed to me, and then she deftly executes what's commonly known in the club scene, I think, as a "slut drop," bending her knees and gyrating her pelvis, moving closer and closer to the floor before snapping back up and pushing her buttocks into my groin.

"Beatrice. Stop."

"What? We're *dancing*." She grabs my wrists and places my hands on her narrow hips, pushing her tank top up slightly so my palms rest on her skin. I try to pull them away, but she holds them there, grinding against my crotch. "This *is* what you want, isn't it?" She turns around, linking her arms around my neck. My hands stay on her hips, as if they're stuck there, magnetized to her body. Rubbing her pelvis against mine, she says, "Stop pretending, for once. Just go with it. This is—oh." She grins, triumphant. "Oh, my." I push her away from me, a little too hard, and dart for the door. Arthur calls something out to me, laughing. I ignore him.

Out on the sidewalk, I smoke in angry silence and think of the decapitated cat and the disemboweled squirrel until everything is okay again.

FIFTEEN

PROGRAMMED TO RECEIVE

WHEN I finally whisk Beatrice away from the party, she follows me onto the litter-strewn sidewalk, stumbling and giggling as her feet send empty cans and bottles tinkling into the gutter. I light a cigarette, looking around and making sure no one outside of La Poubelle or Birds or the Bourgeois Pig has taken notice of her inebriation. "You need to hold it together," I whisper to her through clenched teeth. "At least until we get to the car."

She blinks, smiling stupidly at me. Pointing at my cigarette, she says, "Can I have one?"

I glance over my shoulder at the Scientology Celebrity Centre across the street, enshrouded in darkness. I think I can see men in black clothes roaming about on the lawn behind the fence, but it might be my imagination. "Not out here," I say to Beatrice. "Someone might think badly of it. I'll give you one in the car."

She nods and says, "Are you taking me home now?" Her words are so slurred I can barely understand her.

"No. I'm taking you back to my place. You need to sleep this off. I can't take you back to your parents like this. I'll call your mother and . . . I don't know, I'll make something up."

"Ooh, we're gonna have a *slumber party?*" She stumbles forward and tries to grab my crotch.

Evading her, I take her arm and start leading her toward Tamarind. "Stop that shit," I whisper, my teeth clenched. "There are people out here."

When we get to my car, my heart sinks. The first thing I see is the blue and white car idling next to mine. The flashers on its roof blaze blood-orange. A tall, lanky man in a uniform is leaning against my bumper. *I'm fucked,* I think to myself. *It's all over. I'm going to go down for Arthur's debauchery, and he'll emerge unscathed, as always.*

I picture Arthur, standing in a courtroom, coldly denying any knowledge of his nephew's personal affairs. I picture me, in a jail cell, getting fat on carb-filled prison food and gang-raped by hulking lifers with names like Milkshake and Cheddar G. I picture Judy coming to visit me, her hand pressed to the glass partition as she weeps at the sight of my blackened eyes and bloodied lips.

The panic lasts only for a second before I realize it's a parking enforcement vehicle, not a police cruiser. The relief that comes from this is instantaneous but brief because the parking cop is *leaning against my fucking bumper*. It might not be a nice car, but it's *my car*, and this fucker is lounging against it, lazily scrawling in his thick pad of preprinted tickets. A cigarette hangs from his lips, the glow of its ember intensified beneath the shadow of his cap.

I motion to Beatrice to hang back as I approach the parking cop. "You're leaning on my car," I say, kind of impressed at how calm I sound.

He looks up and, to my surprise, smiles widely. *Too* widely. For half a second, his mouth is spread into a nightmarish grin that takes up most of his face. I retreat a faltering step back, my pulse quickening. I rub my eyes, stung by the sweat on my fingertips. When I reopen them, squinting at the man, his face has returned to normal and I regret the last line of coke I'd done in the bathroom before leaving.

"Something wrong, good sir?" the parking cop asks pleasantly, cocking his head. He doesn't *look* like a parking cop; they're usually dowdy and blunt-featured, the castoffs of LA society. Too ugly to work in the Industry but not ugly enough to fry burritos in a taco truck. This man, however, has the ruggedly symmetrical features that wouldn't look out of place in a summer blockbuster, but there's something off about him. His skin has an unnaturally radiant white glow, like a polished pearl, and his fingers are too long. And while it's too dark to tell, I'm pretty sure his irises are black.

"Um, yeah," I say unsteadily, the image of the monstrous smile still burned into my brain. "Yeah, something's wrong. You're leaning on my car. And you're writing me a ticket even though I'm obviously parked legally."

"*Well,*" says the parking cop, twirling his pen between his impossibly long fingers. "You *were* parked legally. *But . . .*" He jerks his thumb at a sign posted a few yards away and, with an extravagant flourish, shoots his arm out to glance at his watch—a Roger Dubuis, no less. "As of *six minutes ago*, you are *now* parked *il*legally."

"You're going to write me a ticket for six minutes?"

"Precisely. Or, at least—" he waves his pad "—I was *trying* to, until I was so *rudely* interrupted." He looks past me at Beatrice and says, "Is your father always so *brusque* with law enforcement officers?"

"Parking cops are hardly law enforcement officers," I scoff. "And I'm not her father."

He smiles again—a normal-sized smile, thank fuck—and his eyes twinkle with something like knowingness. "No," he says. "I suppose not." He returns his cool gaze to Beatrice. "Is this man giving you any trouble, little darling? Because if he is, I can certainly get on my radio and have a quote-unquote *real* law enforcement officer here in a spec- *tacular* jiffy." His eyes flick black to me, and all the jocular friendliness is gone. I feel, with a cold shiver, that he knows everything about me. Not only about what I've been privy to with Beatrice, and the girls be- fore her, but *everything*. The dead flowers, the feather duster, the yel- low woman who comes at night—he can see all of it, I'm certain.

Startling me out of my terrified trance, Beatrice appears beside me and takes my hand. She squeezes it and smiles at the parking cop. "No," she says. "He's not giving me any trouble at all. But *you* are." I'm amazed at how sober she sounds. She falters a bit at the end, her words sounding a little slippery and loose, but it's almost impossible to tell and

I'm certain the parking cop hadn't caught it. He couldn't have.

For the briefest moment, an expression of dumb shock passes over the parking cop's face, but it's quickly replaced with that wickedly genial grin. He points his pen at Beatrice and says, "I *like* you. Not as much as *he* does, but I admire your style. You've got *spirit*. Spunk. *Pizazz*. Do watch yourself, though, would you? Stockholm's a hell of a syndrome." He goes back to scribbling on his pad. I'm about to say something, but he tears off the top sheet and hands it to me. Glaring at him, I crumple it up without looking at it and drop it on the ground. He stares at it for a few seconds before shrugging and saying, "Hey, man, whatever. It's *your* bench warrant." He turns on his heel and walks over to his own car in long, elegant strides, and I notice he's wearing cowboy boots hued the same eerie white of his skin.

"Wait," I call after him, dismayed by the weak hoarseness of my voice. He turns back to me with his eyebrows raised. "Do I know you?" I ask.

The smile returns—the *bad* smile, seeming to swallow up his whole face. It's there for an even shorter duration than it had been before, but this time, I'm sure I didn't imagine it, coke or no coke. "Better than you think," he says. With a tip of his cap, he winks, gets into his car, and drives off.

"That was really weird," Beatrice says. All the slurry languor in her voice she'd so effectively disguised has returned in full force.

"Did you . . . did you see . . . ?"

She looks up at me, swaying. "See what?" she asks. "Everything is actually kind of . . . *blurry*." She says "blurry" like the word itself has evoked a bemused wonder in her.

I shake my head. "Nothing, don't worry about it," I say distantly. I bend down and pick up the crumpled ticket, flattening it against my palm. I frown.

"What's wrong?" Beatrice asks. "Is it a lot?" She giggles. "You could have *Uncle Arthur* take care of it for you."

I shake my head again, not paying attention to her. It is, in fact, not a parking ticket, at all; it's a plain sheet of paper upon which the parking cop—if that's what he even is—has written in ornate lettering, "*We are programmed to receive.*" Beneath that, a phone number. Beneath the phone number, a horrifically accurate drawing of the yellow woman's wrinkled, wretched face.

All the warmth leaves my body in an arctic rush.

"Ty, what's *wrong?* Are you shaking, or is the world . . . vibrating?" She giggles some more.

I probably would have stood there all night, petrified by that ghastly image I had more or less thought only existed in my head, but then Beatrice reaches for the paper. I whip it back and stuff it into my hip pocket, doing my best to shake off the fear and bury it as deep as it will go. "Nothing," I say. "It's nothing. Come on, let's get out of here."

A steady rain has begun to fall.

• • •

Beatrice falls asleep on the way to my apartment. In some uncommon instance of benevolent Fates, I find a great parking spot on Sunset, a brief walk from the front door to my building. When we get out, Beatrice pukes on the sidewalk. I hold her hair back. A homeless woman watches from the shadows, whispering.

Once inside, I lay her on my futon and cover her with a blanket. She passes out almost instantly. I sit in my desk chair, watching her sleep and trying to think of what I'm going to tell her mother. It's almost one a.m.

Once I think I have my story straight, I put my bathroom trashcan beside the futon in case Beatrice has to throw up again, and then I walk out of the apartment and down the hall to the balcony. The rain has slowed to a modest drizzle. Leaning against the railing, I light a cigarette and call Beatrice's mother.

She answers on the second ring. "Mr. Seward," she gushes. "Oh, sorry—*Ty*. How did it go? You two must be having *quite* a time." Her voice is clear and alert, so I don't think she'd been asleep. I don't love the unsubtle insinuation burbling beneath her words.

"Um. Yeah, everything is ... great," I say, looking down at the trickle of cars on Sunset. "But, uh, I actually called you to tell you—"

"Hmm, let me *guess*. She drank herself stupid and now she's sleeping it off at your place?"

Taken aback, my response isn't what it should be. "What?" I say. "Um, no, no, definitely not. It's ... um ... It's nothing like that. It's just that, um, well—"

"Mr. Seward—*Ty*—please, don't hurt yourself. I know my daughter. Moderation is not something she specializes in. Oh, God, *please* tell me she didn't embarrass herself or say something stupid to somebody important."

"Um. I . . . what?" I shake my head, rubbing my eyes with my thumb and forefinger. "No, um, no, she . . . she didn't."

Her sigh of relief is so loud and so elongated it sounds for a moment like she's stepped outside into a wind storm. "Thank *heavens*," she says. "You'd tell me if she did, right? You can tell me, Mr. Sew—Ty. You can tell me. I want us to have that kind of relationship, okay? No secrets."

Down below, a homeless man is rapping his cardboard sign against the window of a Range Rover idling at the stoplight. I watch, distracted. "Yeah," I say slowly. "No, yeah, for sure. Totally. No . . . secrets."

"Good, good, that makes me very happy. Now, we're in luck because Eric happens to be out of town, so I won't have to spin a yarn for him. If he *were* here . . . well, you and I might be in a spot of trouble."

Her conspiratorial use of "you and I" makes me feel slimy.

"Now, Ty, I want you to *know*—I'm not a prude. I understand how things work. So, if you and Beatrice—well, *you know*—please know that it's fine. My husband disagrees, of course, but don't worry about him. He's stuck in some other time that never even existed. It'll be our little secret."

I clear my throat. "Mrs. Rider—"

"Mm-mm, none of that. It's 'Francesca' to you. No, better yet, call me 'Fran.'"

"Yes, well, *Fran* . . . look, it's not like that."

"No, no, of *course* it's not." I can hear her smiling through the phone. "I know how careful you men have to be nowadays. Especially if you're straight and white. Don't worry, I speak the language. I know the code. It's okay, you don't have to say it. Like I said, it's fine."

"Mrs. Rider—Fran—really, I—"

"Just drop her by sometime tomorrow, okay? No rush. Sleep in. *Enjoy* yourselves."

I sigh. All I can say is, "Okay." It comes out weak, defeated, mouse-like and squeaky.

She says goodbye in a sing-song voice, and I hang up. After I finish my cigarette, I smoke a second one, and a third. When I go back inside, I sit in my desk chair and put my head on my writing desk and try to sleep.

SIXTEEN

BURNING THE RICHES

I wake up on the futon the next morning, sunlight seeping in through the blinds. Beatrice is snuggled against me, her leg curled over my waist and her arm around my neck. Her breath is hot in my ear. I'm fully clothed, but she's stripped to her bra and panties. The blanket has been kicked off us. I have an erection pressing against Beatrice's thigh.

I bolt upright so fast I tumble off the futon and onto the hard floor. Beatrice wakes up, blinking sleepily at me. She looks down at her body, then at me, her eyes lingering on the bulge in the crotch of my jeans. "Good morning," she says, smiling, her voice throaty. "Did we . . ." She trails off, slipping her hand down the front of her panties, checking.

"Jesus, fuck, *no*," I say. "Jesus. Of course not. No."

"Did you take my clothes off, or did I?"

"That's a ridiculous question."

Her grin widens. "Is it ridiculous because you took them off, or because I did?"

"Because you did. Stop playing games."

"Oh, lighten up, I'm messing with you." She stands and pulls on her shorts. The motion apparently has an unpleasant effect on her because she sits right back on the futon instead of putting on her shirt. She groans and says, "Wow. I don't feel so great." She puts her elbows on her knees and rubs her temples.

"Are you going to throw up again?"

She shakes her head, wincing. "No, but do you have some Tylenol, or something?"

I go to my single cabinet above my tiny countertop and rummage around until I find a bottle of Advil. Shaking four tablets into my palm, I grab a Dasani from my minifridge and bring it and the pills to Beatrice. "Have you ever been hung over before?" I ask her.

"A few times, but I always forget how bad it is." She tosses the Advil back and gulps half the water, the bottle crinkling as it drains. "So," she says, wiping her mouth, "how did you end up in bed with me?"

"I . . . don't know. I'm . . . sorry about that."

"Why?"

"Why what?"

"Why are you sorry?" She looks up at me, and I can smell the stale alcohol mixed unpleasantly with her morning breath.

"Because it's inappropriate."

"You keep saying that. 'Inappropriate.' Like any of this whole thing is *appropriate*."

"What whole thing?"

"You know." She shrugs, taking another big gulp from the water bottle. "This whole thing."

"Put your shirt on," I tell her.

"You're so squeamish. You act like you've never seen a woman in a bra before."

"You're not a woman."

"That's not what my mom said when she taught me how to mastur-bate." She pauses, studying me, looking for a reaction I don't give her. "I was eleven, in case you were wondering."

"I wasn't. Put your shirt on. I have to take you home."

• • •

Sitting at the stoplight at Sunset and Van Ness, the car cowering be-neath the ominous presence of the Netflix building, I reach into my back pocket and take out the wad of twenties and fifties Arthur had given me before Beatrice and I had left. "Here," I say, handing the cash to Be-atrice. "This is from Arthur. It's for . . . um, the pizza thing." She takes the money and fans it out, looking at it oddly. The windshield wipers flick back and forth, punctuating the silence between us with whining squeaks.

The light turns green, and my tires spin on the rain-slickened road before the car lurches forward, spraying water. Beatrice collapses the fan of money back into a rectangular stack and runs her fingers along its edges. As I veer off Sunset and onto the 101, she takes my Zippo from the center console and flicks it open. Before I can grasp what she's doing, she lights the stack on fire. I curse at her, grabbing for the flaming money and swerving into the adjacent lane. Someone honks at me. I return both hands to the steering wheel to correct my course, and Beatrice rolls the window down and tosses the money out onto the highway. In my mirror, I watch as dozens of burning bills flutter in the gray sheets of windy rain. Beatrice lights a cigarette.

"That was a lot of money," I say.

Shrugging, she says, "What's a fourteen-year-old going to do with two grand?"

"I could think of a lot of things you could do."

"I guess that's the difference between you and me." She hits the cigarette and holds it up to her face, examining it. "Why do you smoke such shitty cigarettes?" she asks.

"I don't know. I . . . like them."

"Is it, like, a family thing? Your aunt smokes them, too."

"Does she?" I ask, surprised. I've never paid attention to what Aunt Carlotta smokes. "How do you know that?"

"I saw her smoking at the party we went to, at Arthur's house."

"Oh. Okay. Whatever. I don't see why it matters what kind of cigarettes I like."

"It's just kind of a weird cigarette brand to like."

"Well, when you're twenty-one you can buy whatever kind of cigarettes you want."

The look she gives me is one of playful amusement. "Geeze, ease up, tiger. Why are you so tense?"

"I'm not," I say, my hands tightening around the steering wheel.

"Have you ever considered, like, seeing a shrink, or something? I mean, you really need to lighten up."

"My ex is always telling me I should see one," I say, turning onto the 710. "I ignore her."

"Maybe you shouldn't ignore her. You have to do something. You're the most uptight person I know. When's the last time you got laid?"

"That's none of your business."

"See what I mean? That, right there—I ask you a simple question, and you fly off the handle."

Images of all the homeless people I've beaten near to death flash into my head. I remember face-fucking a college girl so hard she threw up on my cock. Another girl who cried when I fisted her because I'd dipped my hand in lemon juice. "You have no idea what me flying off the handle looks like," I tell her.

Not detecting the gravity of my tone, Beatrice says, "Don't threaten me with a good time."

"Nothing about me is a good time." Once, about two weeks into my radiation treatment, I'd gone on a date with a girl and put emetics and laxatives in her soup while she was in the bathroom. I left her at the hospital later that night. "You don't even know."

"Maybe I want to know."

There was a time I gave a girl a baggie of powdered laundry detergent and told her it was crystal meth.

One girl, I shoved a dead goldfish in her vagina before fucking her. Afterward, I took the fish out and made her eat it. To my credit, I microwaved it first.

"I promise you," I say. "You don't want to know."

$$\bullet \ \bullet \ \bullet$$

I don't walk Beatrice to her door when we arrive at her house. She regards me imploringly. I look at my lap, light a cigarette.

"When will I see you again?" she asks.

Raising my head, I stare at the lawns along the quiet suburban street, the grass slick and shining from the rain. How quaint it all is. How fake. "I don't know," I say. "I don't know if you even will. There's . . . not really a reason for you to see me, now that the commercial has been shot." I glance at her, but the expression on her face makes me look away again.

"Well," Beatrice says, sighing. "I mean, we should hang out sometime. Or something."

"Beatrice," I say, measuring my tone, trying not to sound too cold but, in such an effort, sounding too warm, instead.

"Will you text me, at least?"

"That wouldn't be—"

"Appropriate, right, I know. But still."

"Take care of yourself, Beatrice."

"*I'll* text *you*."

Before I can respond, she gets out of the car and hurries up the driveway, carelessly splashing through puddles. I don't wait for her to get to the door before I speed off.

For a while, I'm convinced a black Accord is following me, but I manage to lose it on the 101. Nevertheless, I keep checking for it in my rearview mirror for the duration of the drive home.

SEVENTEEN

OLD BEHAVIOR

THAT night, I pick up an eighteen-year-old model at the bar next door to my apartment building. She looks so much like Beatrice when she first walks in, I think she *is* Beatrice. Honestly, though, that doesn't mean anything. The model doesn't look like Beatrice; Beatrice looks like every other girl in this city.

That's what I tell myself, anyway.

The girl does the whole hard-to-get thing at first, telling me she's waiting for her boyfriend to arrive. I keep at her for five or ten minutes, but when the casual rebuffs start to grate on my nerves, I play my instant-win card and tell her I'm Arthur Seward's assistant. The family relation doesn't matter; it never does. All these girls care about is that I have some sort of professional relationship with Doctor Law. Once they know that—once they think I can *get* them something—they're mine.

The boyfriend is eliminated from the equation. We go to a bar down the street so we won't run into him. The model becomes handsy, flirtatious, trying way too hard. I notice a guy with a blond crewcut watching us, sick with envy, and it fills me with godlike pride.

After the third drink, the model agrees with an excess of enthusiasm to come back to my place. There's not a lot of talk or foreplay. She knows the score. When she undresses, I notice she has a navel ring in the shape of a butterfly. It's distracting, detracting from the fantasy, so I tell her to take it out. She obeys. They always obey.

She starts going down on me, but I can't get hard so I take some used Q-tips out of the bathroom trashcan and force her to eat them. When I still can't get an erection, I make her eat the rest of the trashcan's contents—mainly some snotty Kleenex, paper towels with facial hair and shaving cream and dots of blood on them, a handful of toenail clippings, and a wad of toilet paper I'd wiped with earlier this week but couldn't flush because the toilet hadn't been working.

As I sit there and watch this girl eat garbage because she thinks it's going to somehow help her career, the only thing I feel is bored apathy. LA girls' willingness to debase themselves is tiresome. For once, I wish one of them would stand in indignation and vehemently refuse to comply with my sordid demands. If Beatrice were here, would *she* eat garbage? I doubt it. But if *Arthur* told her to do it? I think she would, but her reasons would be different. With Beatrice, I think everything is a little more complicated than it usually is.

"What now, Daddy?" the model asks, lifting her head from the trashcan and wiping bits of toilet paper from her mouth and cheeks, trying not to throw up.

"Don't call me 'Daddy,'" I tell her. I look around the apartment. My cock is still flaccid, so I have her suck on it some more. When it gets semi-hard, I open the refrigerator and have her stick her head inside while I try to fuck her asshole, but the hole is too tight so I give up, telling her she's going to need to work on that if she wants to get anywhere in this town.

Defeated, I tell the girl to go clean my toilet with her tongue, and then I sit on the futon and check my phone. There's a text from Beatrice: *what r u doing??* I look over at the girl, whose head is submerged in the toilet bowl, and decide not to answer.

EIGHTEEN

REASONS TO BE GOOD

"Y OU'VE slept with someone," Judy said to me late one night, toward the end of our relationship as we had known it for so long. Less than a month had passed since my diagnosis. Certain events would eventually bring us together again—her complicated relationship with her future husband, the quiet hell of my lonely existence—but never in the same capacity.

I was standing at her living room window in the dark, looking out at the hills and the lights in the distance, and the intermittent bursts of traffic below. I held my drink tightly in my hand, like it was everything in the world. I could feel her standing in the bedroom doorway, but I couldn't look at her.

"There's no use denying it," she said, her voice strangely lacking emotion. There was no hurt or venom in her tone. Just stony matter-of-factness. "You always get a certain way after sex. That moody pensiveness, or whatever. It's weird. It's unmistakable. And *I* haven't had sex with you tonight."

I brought the glass to my lips and drained half its contents. "No," I said. "You haven't."

"You're not going to deny it?"

"You told me not to." I shut my eyes and thought of the girl. She'd been seventeen, and a cheerleader—I have a thing for cheerleaders. They have those legs. Judy is beautiful, but she had never had those legs.

"*Why?* How *could* you?" And there it was. The hurt, the venom.

Her questions didn't warrant an answer; I don't even think she was looking for one, but I *had* to answer. I *wanted* to. I needed to hear myself say it. Maybe hearing it, I thought, would help it start to become clearer to me.

"I'm . . . mixed up," I said. "I used to have all these reasons to be good, to do the right thing, to be what I was expected to be. There was so much in my life that *mattered*, and now it's all gone. Nothing matters, nothing makes sense. Everything is fucked." I waited for her to say something. I waited a long time, but she was silent, so I continued. "Everything is fucked," I said again, "and there are things I want to feel that I haven't felt in a long time, because it might be my last chance."

"Things like *what?*" Judy whisper-hissed. "Never mind, it doesn't matter. It's *not* your last chance, you're—"

"It *does* matter. It matters a whole goddamn hell of a lot." I swallowed the rest of my drink and turned to her. She was enshrouded in shadow, but I knew she was crying. "With you, in the beginning, there

115

was this . . . this rush. This excitement. You know what I'm talking about. It's like—"

"It's like being young and giddy," Judy half-choked through her tears. "I know it. I still feel it. With *you*. I feel it every day."

"I don't," I said. "I haven't felt it for a long time." I turned back to the window and added, "Not with you."

From the corner of my eye, I saw her put her face in her hands and slide down against the door frame, curling into a ball and letting her sobs envelop her. I yearned for the desire to go to her, to comfort her, but I didn't have it. All I could do was stand there and let her cry.

NINETEEN

COUNTING DOWN

A couple of months glide languidly by. The gloomy June skies give way to perpetual July-and-August sunshine much more befitting of LA's aesthetic. I help Arthur cast another couple of commercials—one for a new brand of expensive vodka, another for luxury lingerie—and the girls he hires aren't anything like Beatrice. They're a little older, for one—sixteen or seventeen, I think—but not anywhere near as intelligent or sprightly. They are, on the contrary, vapid and vacuous, little more than insipid, brainless fame-whores. Arthur makes me leave the room this time when he fucks them.

The after-hours shoots are relatively tame, all things considered. With the vodka girl, it's mainly her reclining on a fake cloud while masturbating with the neck of the bottle, the brand's label in full view of the camera. The lingerie girl's shoot is pretty much a run-of-the-mill porno, with her wearing different articles of lacy undergarments while getting fucked in various positions by a succession of increasingly burly men.

When we're not doing commercials, I'm following Arthur around to countless meetings with lawyers and studio executives and politicians, taking notes he rarely even glances at and doing my best to "be invisible, yeah?"

I send my *Romeo and Juliet* script to a few underling contacts I've surreptitiously made at some of the studios, but my hopes are measured, if not altogether nonexistent.

The night sweats worsen.

The yellow woman keeps coming.

I feel like I'm on the brink of something catastrophic, as though my life is suspended from the ticking second hand on a timer attached to a roll of dynamite. Every day, the ticking grows louder. Everything hangs in the balance, at the mercy of something horrible and unseen.

Sometimes, at night, I'll drive to the Griffith Observatory and stand on the terrace, looking out over the expansive, brightly-lit cityscape. High above the noise and the filth, away from all the dereliction and destitution, I can almost pretend Los Angeles is everything I want it to be. Swathed in twinkling golden light, quiet and serene, it's almost like it isn't killing me.

But then I'll drive back down the hill, descending once again into the grime, where the sounds of traffic are a constant, metallic whine and the deranged shrieks of the homeless carry on through the night. Where the sidewalks are streaked with shit and cluttered with knocked-over electric scooters. Where the curbs are overflowing with garbage and abandoned furniture, and where the smell of pot smoke is an ominous, omnipresent force.

And I'll let myself into my cramped, overpriced closet of an apartment, going to sleep to the endless sounds of sirens and car horns, and I'll think to myself, *I'm meant for something better.*

TWENTY

A CERTAIN KIND OF SADNESS

I wake up one Friday night in the middle of August to find the yellow woman on top of me. She's rubbing her clammy, callused hands over my face, my neck, my chest, whispering garbled secrets in my ear. When I start screaming, she leaps off me and scurries, on all fours, back into the closet. Shivering, with hot tears stinging my eyes, I hurriedly get dressed, grab my phone and cigarettes, and go out onto the balcony, hoping no one is there. It's past midnight, but a few of my neighbors often sit out there into the early hours of morning, drinking beer and getting stoned. Tonight, mercifully, it's empty.

I sit against the railing and try to light a cigarette, but my hands are trembling and I drop my lighter. It clangs through the metal slats, bounces off the second-floor balcony below, and plummets to the sidewalk. The tears are flowing freely now, and a sob is building in my chest. I can't keep living like this.

I unlock my phone and stare at the home screen, wanting to talk to someone but not knowing whom. Judy would be the most obvious choice, but there's the husband to worry about. Allison is out of the question because we don't have that kind of relationship. Arthur would laugh at me, tell me to lay off the drugs. Aunt Carlotta would be gravely concerned and convince Arthur to lock me up in a psych hospital.

Before I'm aware of what I'm doing, I select Beatrice's contact. The phone is ringing in my ear. When she answers, her voice is groggy but relatively clear. "This is a weird surprise," she says. I hear her yawn. "Do you, like, make a habit of blowing girls off for months and then calling them at twelve-thirty at night?"

I open my mouth to speak, but nothing comes out. I keep thinking of the yellow woman, waiting for me in her shadows, and it makes speech impossible.

"You missed my birthday, you know," says Beatrice. "You could have at least texted me a gif, or something. I know you know it, because it's in my paperwork."

I try to remember the date of her birthday, try to picture the space, midway down the page on the second sheet of legal forms, where it would have been, but I can't. There's only the yellow woman's face, leering and laughing.

"What even is this, some sort of booty call?" Beatrice asks, yawning again. "Because, let me tell you, that ship has totally sailed."

I again try to speak, but I'm horrified when all that comes out is a harsh, barking sob.

"Ty?" she says, her tone raising in what I guess is concern. "What's wrong?"

Summoning all my will, I'm able to choke out the words, "Beatrice. I'm . . . scared."

"Of what? What's going on?" I can picture her sitting up in bed, gripping her phone tighter.

"You . . . wouldn't believe me," I manage to say, taking a shuddering breath.

"I think you'd actually be surprised by the things I'm willing to believe."

Taking another breath, I shut my eyes and bow my head. "I can't . . . I can't go back in my . . . apartment," I whisper. "I can't go back in there."

"Why? What's in there?"

"I can't . . . tell you. But I can't go in there."

"Ty. You're scaring me. Please, what's going on?"

"It's been going on for a long time. Ever since I was a kid."

"You're not making any sense." She pauses. "Ty, I'm sorry, but . . . have you been—"

"No. I'm not drunk. I haven't had anything to drink."

"What about—"

"No. Nothing."

"Okay." She pauses again, this time for much longer. "Listen," she finally says, her voice quiet, "maybe you should . . . come over. Just to, like, talk. You're obviously upset, and if you can't go in your apartment . . ."

I don't tell her that would be inappropriate. I don't tell her I'm an adult and she's a kid. I tell her, "I don't think . . . your parents . . ." I trail off.

"They're not here," she says. "My dad's supposedly on a business trip, but he's probably fucking some girl. And my mom is in Palm Springs for the weekend doing . . . honestly, I don't even know. Something. Neither of them will be back till Monday."

"They left you there . . . alone?"

"Well, I'm fifteen, so."

Sighing raggedly, I say, "If I come over, it's not for—"

"God, Ty, stop. I know. Look, I never *actually* wanted to do anything with you. I just liked to, I don't know, get a rise out of you, you know? I was goofing around. It's not even a thing."

"I just need someone to talk to."

"Yeah, I can tell. Bring some cigarettes, though. My mom forgot to leave me some."

• • •

She answers the door wearing a fluffy pink bathrobe, her hair piled in a messy bun atop her head. She hugs me, which I at first resist, then awkwardly return. She leads me into the living room, where there's a bottle of scotch and two tumblers sitting on the coffee table. She pours us each a glass, handing one of them to me. I down it in a single swig and sit on the couch. She sits beside me, preserving a modest amount of space between us. "So," she says, taking a small sip from her own glass. "Are you ready to tell me what's going on?"

I pour myself some more scotch, knock it back, and refill the glass. My hands haven't stopped shaking.

"Easy, there, tiger," Beatrice says.

"I don't know where to start," I say, cupping my glass in both hands, trying to will the shivers to stop.

"Well, you said you can't go in your apartment. You said there's something in there. Why don't you start by telling me what it is?"

I swallow and look across the room into the cold, black deadness within the hearth. "It's . . . It's a . . ." I can't bring myself to say it. I've never said it out loud.

"It's a what? A mouse? Because my dad has some–"

"It's a woman. It's a terrible woman." The statement hangs there between us, coiling and twisting like a snake.

"A . . . woman?" Beatrice says. "Like, someone you're . . . sleeping with?"

I grimace, shake my head. "No. Not that kind of woman."

"Oh." She shivers, takes a long sip of her scotch. Whispering, she says, "Are we, like, talking about a . . . ghost?"

"Sort of. I don't know. I don't know if she's even . . . real. But I think she is." Shaking my head again, I say, "No. That's not true. I know she's real."

"Who is she?"

"I don't know. I don't know who she is. Sometimes, I almost know. Sometimes I'm so close to knowing, but then it's gone."

Beatrice nods slowly, circling her finger around the rim of her glass. "And . . . what does she, like, *do*? What does she look like?"

My voice low and unsteady, I tell her, "She's wrinkly and yellow, the color of nicotine stains, and she has long, stringy white hair. She's naked, she's always naked, and she smells like stale cigarettes." I stop, taking several long breaths. My heart is hammering against my chest, like a prisoner slamming his fists against his confines. "She only comes at night. I'll wake up, and she'll be there, standing in the corner. Sometimes, she just watches me. Other times, she . . . she touches me."

"Criminy," Beatrice whispers. "Is this . . . every night?"

"Not every night. But most nights."

"Ty . . ." Her face is so full of empathetic pain and compassion, I could start crying all over again.

"I want it to stop," I say, worried I *am* going to start crying again. "I want her to leave me alone." It's happening—a tear escapes my eye, followed by another. I look away, sick with shame.

"Ty," Beatrice says again. She sets her glass on the table and scoots closer to me. She pulls me to her, and I bury my face in the soft shoulder of her robe and sob in a way I haven't in . . . I don't know, probably my entire life. She strokes my hair, and I clutch her and cry for a long time.

It feels embarrassing, it feels pathetic, but it also feels cathartic, like coming home after being gone for a long time.

When there's nothing left, I lift my head, wiping my face on the sleeve of my shirt. I look at Beatrice, and it's as though she's become something else. She's not a fifteen-year-old girl anymore—she's nothing material at all, but an abstraction, an ethereal embodiment of all my wasted hopes and dreams, of all the things I've ever desired, but that Los Angeles has steadfastly refused to grant me. She seems to radiate a golden light—the same light that glitters across the city at night when it's viewed from high above.

Seeing something in my face, Beatrice gives me a look and says softly, "Ty, don't. That's not what you want."

But it is. In this moment, she is everything I want.

"Ty," she says, her tone a warning, like she's addressing a dog that's considering snatching a scrap of food from the dinner table. "You're upset and you're confused, and you don't want—"

I don't let her finish. My mouth is upon hers, insisting she's wrong. My kiss informs her of all the things I'm unable to put into words.

She resists lightly at first, not pulling away, but not returning the kiss, either. In the current between us, I can feel her brain working. My hands slide up her arms and go to her hair, undoing the bun so it falls in a cascade around her face, and all at once she's kissing me back, pushing against me, parting her lips. Our tongues meet, and the electricity could bring the whole city to its knees.

It goes on for a few minutes, the two of us breathless in our consumption of each other, until she pulls away, gasping for air, and says, "Ty. Are you sure . . . is this really—"

I'm upon her again, kissing her neck, my hand slipping inside her robe and pressing against her clavicle. She moans, her fingernails digging into my scalp, and she says, "No, Ty, not here." She gets up and takes my hand, pulling me up the stairs and into her bedroom. Standing before me, she unfastens her robe and lets it fall to the floor around her ankles.

I've seen her in all various stages of undress, but something is different this time. Her body, garbed only in silk white panties, is like some holy marriage of youth and womanhood. There is no perversion in her nudity, and when I go to her, I am without shame.

Being inside of her is like being on an open road with a full tank of gas and nowhere to be, the arms of the horizon spread open to receive you as the rolling sky beckons you forward. It's a freedom unlike any other. It's a release. It's forgiveness.

In bed with her, her body moving against me, her soft, gasping moans filling my ears, I think to myself, *If this is all LA has to give me, maybe everything else was entirely worth it.*

TWENTY-ONE
BROKEN PIECES

I wind up spending the rest of the weekend with Beatrice. There's no more talk of the yellow woman, and if she's followed me to the big Tudor house in San Marino, she doesn't make her presence known.

When we're not in bed, we're in her swimming pool or sunning ourselves on the pool deck or watching movies in the living room. At night, I take her to fancy restaurants I can't exactly afford, charging the bill to my rarely used credit card. I eat only light salads and soups—never more than four hundred calories—but if Beatrice finds this odd, she doesn't say anything. We stay up late, smoking by the pool and talking. It feels good, talking to her. Now that I've recategorized her in my mind, shifting her role from Off-limits Child to She's *Basically* an Adult and I'm Sleeping with Her, I'm able to more fully appreciate how intelligent she is. She's a skilled and pleasant conversationalist, and not since my early days with Judy has there been someone in my life to whom I enjoyed talking. I'd forgotten what it was like to have a friend, and I hadn't realized how total and all-consuming my isolation was until Beatrice pierced it.

Sunday night, we're sitting naked by the pool with our feet dangling in the water, smoking cigarettes after a protracted bout of lovemaking, when Beatrice asks me, "Why don't you have a girlfriend?"

I look at the moonlight splayed across the still water, trying to figure out if I should lie. Ultimately, I decide there's no point in withholding the truth, so I tell her, "Technically, I do. Sort of. But it's not anything serious."

I feel her eyes on me, but I don't look over at her. "How old is she?" she asks.

"Why is that important?"

"I don't know. I'm just curious."

I sigh, tapping ash onto the ground beside me. A sudden breeze sweeps it into the pool. "She's sixteen. Well, she'll be seventeen next month." I pause. "I . . . think." I peek at Beatrice out of the corner of my eye, but I can't read her expression.

"Was she also one of . . . Arthur's girls?"

Grimacing, I shake my head and say, "Shit, no. It's nothing like that. You're the first of 'Arthur's girls' that I've–" I swallow, coughing into my fist "–slept with."

"Gee, I don't know if that should make me feel special, or . . ." She shrugs. "I don't know."

"I don't think it should make you feel anything."

"How did you meet her, then?"

Stubbing out my cigarette, I light another one and say, "There was this party at her house in Bel Air. Her dad was co-financing some movie Arthur was involved with. She approached me, not the other way around." I shrug. "I guess you could say she was pretty . . . forward." I look over at Beatrice, trying to gauge her reaction. Her brow is furrowed, her lips pursed.

"That's . . . kind of weird," she says.

I raise my eyebrows. "Weird? You're not much younger than she is."

She shakes her head. "No, not the age thing. I mean, why would she approach you?"

"I'm . . . not following."

"Like, obviously, you're hot. But, no offense, what do you have to offer her? You're just the assistant." She winces at her own words and gives me an apologetic look. "Shit, I'm sorry, I didn't mean for it to come out like that. That's not how I meant it."

"It's fine," I say, looking down at my cigarette. "But you'd be surprised what 'just the assistant' can get you when the guy you work for is Arthur Seward. Either way, it wasn't like that. She doesn't need anything from me."

"No, that's what I mean. I know all about kids who live in Bel Air. There's nothing you could get her that her daddy couldn't get her."

"So? I don't see your point."

She finishes her cigarette and lies on her side, propping her head up with her hand and looking at me contemplatively. "My point is . . . what's her, like, angle?"

"Who says she has an angle?"

The look she gives me is so wise it's almost condescending. "Ty. It's LA. Everyone has an angle. I think you know that better than most people."

I'm feeling uneasy. I've never given my relationship—if that's even what it could be called—with Allison a whole lot of thought, but now I'm thinking, why *haven't* I thought about it? Is it because there's nothing to think about, or is it because there's something there, simmering beneath the surface, and I don't want to confront it? A familiar fear starts forming at the base of my neck, sending unpleasant chills throughout my body. I look around for the yellow woman, trying to spy her hovering somewhere in the shadows, but I don't see her anywhere.

Something else occurs to me, and I look warily at Beatrice. "Wait, what's *your* angle?"

She laughs. "I mean, honestly? I like how you make me feel." She could leave it at that, but she has to complicate it by adding, "I like that you're just so . . . *sad*. You're this sad, broken guy, and it makes me feel better about how sad and broken I am. It's like your broken pieces fit with my broken pieces, and when I'm with you, I don't feel as broken anymore. It's like I'm all put together, for once."

I stare at her, not sure how to take that. "You don't . . . come across as sad," I say. "Or broken. All things considered, you seem pretty . . . well-adjusted."

She frowns, averting her eyes. "Well, I kinda have to. I have to be what men want, and most men don't want sad, broken girls."

"You don't have to be what anyone wants," I say, and I sound so sincere I almost believe it myself. "That's just some bullshit your crazy mother has sold you."

Beatrice shakes her head solemnly. "No, you're lying. I know how things work. My mom is . . . different, and she's kind of awful, but she knows what she's talking about. Like, don't get me wrong, I wish she wasn't . . . the way she is. Every day I wish that. But I also know she's right. All this feminist stuff that's gotten so popular—it doesn't really *mean* anything. All those girls who are 'empowered,' who are all like, 'down with the patriarchy,' and whatever—they're not going to *get* anywhere. They don't realize we *need* men, and the *real* power comes from using them. Especially if you can make them think *they're* using *you*."

"Is that . . . what this is?" I ask. "Are you just . . . using me?"

She laughs again, but this time there's no humor in it. "Oh, stop. You know I'm not using you like *that*. But, like, isn't everybody just using everybody else, for one thing or another? I guess, I mean . . . in a *way*, yeah, I'm using you to feel better. The same way *you're* using *me* to feel better."

I look at the sky, unable to think of anything to say, because I know she's right.

• • •

I realize something later, lying in bed with her, watching her sleep. I realize, for the first time since Judy, I've involved myself with a girl whom I don't want to hurt or humiliate (I've never done anything weird to Allison, but that's only because I know she probably wouldn't go for it—I've fantasized about it plenty).

Because of this, I pull up Amazon on my phone and start making some purchases.

• • •

Beatrice gives me a bottle of Ambien when I leave on Monday morning. "They're my mom's," she explains, "but she never takes them because she says they make her feel sick. I take one every once in a while, when I can't sleep. They help."

I take the bottle from her and look at it, turning it over in my hand, not saying anything.

"Until we figure out what to do about the yellow woman," Beatrice says.

I nod gravely, secretly pleased she used the word "we." It makes me feel not so alone.

"I don't go back to school for another couple weeks," says Beatrice, "so whenever you're free and you want to hang out, let me know."

"What about your dad?"

Shrugging one shoulder and rolling her eyes, she says, "He's hardly ever here. Besides, my mom pretty much runs the show, and obviously she won't have a problem with it."

"Right," I say, nodding again. "Obviously."

"Text me," she says, kissing me in the doorway. "And take the pills."

• • •

The Ambien helps. I can still sense the yellow woman's presence, but I'm usually knocked out by the time she emerges, and she stops waking me up. Occasionally, I'll catch a glimpse of her darting back into the closet when I open my eyes in the morning, but I can handle that.

Most of the week, I'm busy doing various gofer assignments for Arthur, mind-boggling in their tedium, and I have to attend a few parties in which A-list celebrities pay to watch Mexican kids beat each other to death. Arthur holds a raffle at the end of each fight—the buy-in for which is exorbitant—and the winner gets to have sex with one of the dead kids. If there's a better way to ruin your childhood than watching a popular nineties sitcom actor fuck a hole cut into a dead boy's stomach, I don't know what it is.

Beatrice comes over a couple of nights when I get off early. She's waiting at the end of her driveway each time I pick her up, which I appreciate, because that way I don't have to deal with her mother. I'll take her back to my place and we'll fuck on my futon and watch *It's Always Sunny in Philadelphia* on Hulu, and the yellow woman leaves us alone.

My purchases don't arrive until Thursday because it had been cheaper to buy them from an international third-party seller, but when they do, I'm filled with an anticipation I haven't felt since early-childhood Christmas mornings. I tear open the package and appraise the articles within, deciding, yes, they're exactly what I'd had in mind.

TWENTY-TWO

THE DEEPEST SHADE OF MUSHROOM BLUE

AFTER the diagnosis—and, particularly, after the seventeen-year-old who ended things between me and Judy—I went into a kind of downward spiral. I stopped eating almost entirely and would weigh myself on an almost hourly basis whenever I was at home. Physically, I felt okay; the cancer itself wasn't causing any side-effects, and the radiation that would render me incapable of swallowing was still a couple of months away. I think the reason my eating habits—or profound lack thereof—worsened so substantially was out of some dire desire to exert control over my body. That's what a psychiatrist would have told me, anyway. Whatever it was, it gave me a much-needed sense of superiority. I'd been starving myself for years, but never so successfully. I could look down my nose at all the fat slobs who complained about their "diets" that "didn't work," and at all the fools who were slaves to their own biology. I had conquered biology.

Once, a corpulent friend of Arthur's named Martha had made some comment about how I should "eat a cheeseburger, or something." She didn't know about the diagnosis. Usually, if anyone said anything about how thin I was, I'd tell them, "Well, I have cancer, so." The smug satisfaction I felt when their faces fell never got old. But with Martha, I experimented with a different tactic. I told her, "You know, it's funny that overweight people can say things like 'eat a cheeseburger' to someone who's skinny. They can say it, and no one cares. But if a skinny person says to a fat person something like, say, 'Eat a salad,' or 'Do you *really* think that large fry was the best idea?' or 'Christ, woman, there *is* such a thing as a fucking treadmill,' it would be the end of the fucking world." I paused, watching her face contort, and then I added, "Also, I have cancer." Martha stopped making comments after that.

The self-starvation thing was only the beginning of my transgressions. I soon began drinking myself into unconsciousness every night. I smoked, on average, about three packs of cigarettes a day. I was always sneezing blood from all the shitty coke I was doing pretty much around the clock. I fucked a lot of vapid young women—mostly eighteen- and nineteen-year-olds, but a few high schoolers, as well—and made them do things like eat cigarettes and toothpicks, or masturbate with steel wool. Sometimes, before fucking them, I'd slather the condom in Tabasco sauce. I guess I thought hurting someone else would dampen my own pain—the compulsions were probably driven by the same part of my brain that had compelled me to beat up the homeless kid—but it didn't work. It wasn't what I truly wanted to do, and it left me feeling empty and bored.

There was another element to the sadism, something deeper, some unresolved conflict between my actions and my desires, but I didn't dare explore it.

Judy broke things off with me not long after the night I copped to my infidelity, and the most unfortunate part of that was it meant I had to move out of her Century City high rise and into a shitty little studio on the corner of Sunset and Bronson. I told myself it was temporary, a brief means to an end, but I'm still here. There are many moments—usually when I'm driving in endless circles looking for somewhere to park—in which I wish I'd lied to her.

Then again, I'm not sure I could have. The cancer made me so cold, so apathetic, I can't imagine myself having kept up with the ruse for long, no matter how preferable the living conditions were. There were many nights when I stood at the foot of her bed, looking at her naked body bathed in pale, silver moonlight, wanting so badly to want her but not able to make myself. Sometimes, I could still fuck her if I was able to detach myself enough from my own body, but those occasions had become increasingly infrequent in the end. When it got to the point that our sex life became essentially nonexistent, it was an unspoken point of contention. I could feel the resentment coming off her in waves. Every time she looked at me, I could see all the secret suspicion, fear, and jealousy hiding behind her eyes.

The night before my radiation treatments started, I procured a prostitute. I'd been living on my own for a couple of months, and I called one of Arthur's friends who ran a discreet, high-end escort service. He owed me a favor for some shady business I'd helped him out with some months prior—at Arthur's command, but that didn't matter—and he said it would be on the house as long as I tipped the girl. When I told him to send me the youngest one he had, he said, "My friend, I do not think you know what you are asking for," so I'd told him no, nothing like *that*, she needed to be legal—or close to legal—but I wanted her to look young and innocent. Angelic, if possible. He said it was. He said with him, anything was possible.

The girl showed up at my door in a baby doll dress, her long dark hair neatly brushed and held back with a yellow headband. She smiled. I told her she looked like a child. She said, "Isn't that what you wanted?"

She left an hour later, sobbing, clutching her twenty-dollar tip.

I cried, too, after she departed, but for different reasons.

Arthur's friend called me and told me we were square. No more favors. He told me if I ever made enough money to afford his girls, to please go elsewhere.

I told him that was fine.

TWENTY–THREE

SHAMEFUL YEARNINGS

I go over to Allison's house on Friday afternoon because I haven't seen her in a while and I don't want her to suspect something is amiss—I still might need her dad. She's confused when I tell her I don't feel like having sex, but she doesn't make a big deal out of it. We do some of her coke, and it's pretty decent. She asks me what I've been up to, and I give her a censored recap, leaving out anything about Beatrice or necrophiliac celebrities. She'll ask me for specific details about some of the things I tell her—who was at a certain party, what time I got home from a fundraiser, whom I've sent my script to, where I got coffee in the morning, *et cetera*. I'm in the middle of telling her about a fictitious concert I allegedly went to the other night in order to fill the time slot that had been occupied by Beatrice, when I stop, eyeing her with sudden suspicion. "Hang on," I say. "Why are you so interested in all this?"

I'm lying on her couch, sucking on her Juul while she sits on her bed, painting her toenails. She looks up at me, her expression puzzled. "Huh?" she says.

"Why are you so interested in what I've been doing?"

Allison cocks her head, raising an eyebrow. "Um. Because, like, we're sort of dating, or whatever. I always ask you about what you've been doing."

"You . . . do?" I say, unsure. I try to recall if this is true, but I can't, for the life of me, remember anything we've ever talked about in the eight months we've been together.

"Uh, yeah. Literally, all the time."

"Well . . . why? Why do you . . . care?" I take a long pull from the Juul, studying her.

"Yikes," she says, going back to her nails. "Whatever, never mind."

She doesn't need anything from you.

Everyone has an angle.

"No, seriously," I say, not willing to let this die. "Why do you care who's looking at my script? Or where I get my fucking coffee from? What difference does it make to you?"

Sighing, not looking up from her nails, she answers, "It *doesn't* make a difference to me, honestly. For real, I don't care *what* you do. I'm trying to be nice because I'm a nice person, and if we're not going to bang—and, let's be real, what are you even *doing* here, if we're not?— but *since* we're not going to, I have to fill the time *some*how, so I thought it would be nice of me to at least pre*tend* like I'm interested in the things you do when you're not jerking off with my body."

I blink at her. "Maybe I should . . . go," I say.

She shrugs, leaning closer to her toenails and blowing on them. "Do what you want," she says.

From the car, I call Beatrice and tell her I'll pick her up in an hour.

I'm thinking about the items in the package the whole way there.

• • •

"I have something for you," I'm telling Beatrice as we ascend the stairs of my apartment building. My voice is unsteady, and I'm trembling. I have no idea how she's going to react.

"Something like a present?" she asks. We reach the top of the stairs and walk down the hallway, stopping outside my door. I've begun to perspire.

"Um. Sort of," I say. "But this thing I have for you—these *things*—they're more like a present for me." I unlock the door and open it, hurrying her inside. As soon as the door closes, I relock both locks and turn on the lights.

I've delicately laid my purchases out on the futon, and when I gesture at them, smiling nervously, Beatrice looks long and hard at me, and then at the items. She walks over to the futon and stares at them, lifting them up and inspecting them.

"Ty," she says, "what is this?"

My mouth dry, my throat hoarse, I tell her, "It's all I want. It's what I crave."

"I don't get it."

"Look," I say. "This . . . isn't easy for me."

She walks over to me, her face compassionate, and strokes my arm. "Yeah, I can see that," she says. "Just, like, try and relax. Tell me what you want."

I sit on the futon because I feel like my legs are going to give out. "There are a lot of things I do with girls–things I make *them* do–but it's not what I want. What I want is *this.*" I gesture at the items beside me on the futon. Looking up at Beatrice, I say, "I want to be dominated. I want you to hurt me."

"But . . . I don't *want* to hurt you."

Taking one of her hands in both of mine, I say, "Please. I can't do this with anyone else. You're the only one."

"Why me?"

"Because you're . . . different."

Her eyes drift over to the items. She pulls away from me and approaches them again with exaggerated timidity, like she's advancing upon a sleeping Rottweiler. "So," she says uncertainly, lifting up the corset and the crotchless panties, "you want me to put these on, and these–" she picks up the spiked heels "–and you want me to–" she nods at the riding crop "–like, *hit* you with that?"

I nod, sheepish.

"Criminy," she breathes, biting her lip and shaking her head a little. She picks up the length of rope. "And I'm guessing you want me to tie you up, too?" I nod again. "What about that?" she asks, pointing at the ball gag. I tell her it goes in my mouth.

When she picks up the last item, the image of her holding it is almost too much. I'm flooded with simultaneous, juxtaposed sensations of lust and terror.

"And this?" she asks.

"That . . ." I whisper. "We'll get to that."

DOMINATED

No orgasm was ever so sweet.

TWENTY-FIVE

THE LOUDEST SILENCE

WELL," says Beatrice, dismounting me, "that was . . . weird."

She sets about untying my wrists and ankles, which she'd done an impressively thorough job of knotting. Next, she unfastens the ball gag and gently withdraws it from my mouth. She has a look of revulsion on her face when she extracts the handle of the feather duster from my rectum. She carries it into the bathroom, her heels clicking on the hardwood floor, and I hear it clatter into the bathtub. She comes back with a handful of paper towels and starts wiping the blood from the bleeding welts where she'd struck my torso with the sharp-studded riding crop.

"Was it . . . good for you?" she asks, dabbing at an insistently bleeding spot on my chest, where the riding crop had nicked my nipple.

"It was . . . everything," I pant. "It was everything I . . . always wanted . . . from a girl."

"You gotta tell me, though—what's with the feather duster?"

For half a second, an image springs into my mind of a terrible shadow looming over me, holding a feather duster, whispering, "*There's nothing to fear. I'm just going to show you how to play.*" But as soon as it had come, it's gone.

"I don't . . . really know," I say. I get up, unscrew the smoke detector, and light two cigarettes. I hand one to Beatrice, and we sit beside each other on the futon. "I just . . . like how it feels." I think about it for a second, shake my head, and amend, "No, actually. I *hate* how it feels, but for some reason, that makes it even better."

"Has any other girl done that to you?"

"Before tonight, I've never been . . . dominated. But I did convince my ex to use the feather duster on me. Only once, though. After that one time, she told me to never ask her to do it again."

"I mean, it *is* kind of weird. Not even kind of. It's *really* weird." She looks at me, realizes something, and says, "But, like, if *you* like it, I'll keep doing it. Just . . . not every time?"

"Okay," I agree, kissing her forehead. "Not every time."

• • •

For the duration of the following day, I'm unable to get the image of Beatrice in the dominatrix outfit out of my head. It makes concentration impossible. I have the day off from being Arthur's errand boy, so I'd been planning on touching up my screenplay, but the black words on the screen keep melding together to form the corset, tightly clinging to Beatrice's torso. I masturbate furiously, more times than is worth keeping track of, but there's no release. Each orgasm is painful. The semen stings like battery acid when I squeeze it into clumps of wadded-up Kleenex.

By the afternoon, I can take it no more, so I text Beatrice and sit around waiting for a reply. Five minutes pass. Ten minutes. Twenty. Half an hour. I try masturbating again but my dick is chafed and raw, and I'm all out of moisturizer.

I pick up my phone and try calling her, but it goes straight to voicemail. I've never gotten her voicemail before. She doesn't have a personalized message—it's only the cold, automated, "*The person you are trying to reach...*"—so I'm not even granted the faint relief of hearing her voice.

Hours drag by endlessly. I try watching TV, but it gives me a headache. My phone remains silent.

I feel cold, alone, unplugged from life. I pace my apartment, chain-smoking cigarettes until the air becomes noxious, burning my eyes and my throat, forcing me to leave.

I venture outside into the hot night, where everything somehow feels louder than usual. The car horns are like explosions. The grinding metal of construction machinery seems to signify a coming apocalypse. Overheard snippets of passersby's inane conversations are a smothering, suffocating pillow over my face. I'm cognizant enough to think, *What is wrong with me? What is happening?*

It was the feather duster, the yellow woman answers from somewhere inside me. *You took it too far. You freaked her out. You scared her off.*

I walk up Bronson, trudging through ankle-deep litter, ignoring the bleating pleas of vagrants. I consider beating one of them up, maybe even killing one, but no, not now, not in broad daylight.

I make it to Franklin, which is cleaner and has fewer homeless people, but the ominous stares of the Scientology guards posted around the block are more oppressive than usual, making me want to run and hide. I keep seeing a black Accord I'm pretty sure is following me. I glance over at Guide Bar, and the memory of Beatrice dancing on me, grinding against me, is too much and I have to sit on a bench and steady my breathing. I can feel the yellow woman everywhere, which doesn't make sense because she doesn't come out in public, but the sensation is unmistakable and my eyes keep darting around, attempting to catch her.

I walk into Gelson's, shrinking under the stern gaze of the Scientology guard who's standing outside the entrance with his hands in his pockets. Inside, I wander around for a while, trying to ignore a guy with a blond crewcut who I think might be watching me. I eventually buy a cheap bottle of vodka and, in a last-ditch attempt to make myself feel better, a brand-new feather duster.

Walking home, I keep checking my phone, but Beatrice still hasn't replied. I text her again, which makes me feel pathetic because I *never* double-text girls, and when I get back to my apartment, I try calling her again, but it still goes straight to voicemail.

I resolve to drink half the bottle of vodka, because I haven't eaten anything today and I barely ate yesterday, so I can afford the 800 calories. Something happens, however, and suddenly I've drunk the entire bottle, and the despair at having consumed 1,600 whole calories washes over me in a tidal wave of shame.

I call Beatrice a few more times and keep getting her voicemail, so I chew three Ambien and sit crying on my futon until the blackness inside of me spills out into the world and swallows it whole.

TWENTY–SIX

KY

O N the first day of my final week of radiation treatments, I met a man who told me about God.

I was sitting alone in the strangely empty waiting room, trying to stay awake. Arthur had started having one of his drivers take me to the hospital each day because I was too tired to drive myself, but the driver always waited outside.

It was cold in the waiting room, and I shivered in my seat, sipping a cup of cucumber water and watching an assortment of tropical fish swim in dumb circles in the tank next to the reception desk. After I'd been waiting about fifteen minutes, an old man entered, looking as most elderly cancer patients do—pale, withered, frail, beaten-down. To my (visible, I'm sure) disgust, he sat right beside me, despite having two dozen other empty chairs from which to choose. He crossed his legs, grimacing as he did, and looked at me with big, soulful eyes. "Have you found

God yet?" he asked me.

I blinked tiredly at him, too exhausted to even tell him off, as much as I wanted to—the most annoying thing a stranger can do is stop being an object, part of the scenery, and force itself into your life, crying for your attention.

"If you're here, and you haven't found God," the old man carried on, "you're in some *bad* trouble."

I stared straight ahead at the fish. "If you're here, you're in trouble no matter what," I told him. "God or no God."

The old man laughed, too loudly. "No arguments there, friend," he said, nodding, smiling. His teeth were disgusting. "I think you've misunderstood my meaning, good sir. I'm not saying God will prevent bad things from happening to you. No, sir, I am not saying that at all."

"Great," I said, scratching at my nicotine patch. I wasn't allowed to smoke during the course of the treatment, and guys like this didn't make the forced cessation any easier.

"What I'm *saying*, good sir, is God will *help* you when the bad things *do* happen."

"Is that right."

"It is!" the old man said, nearly shouting, clapping his hands together. The receptionist looked over at us. I tried to communicate telepathically with her, screaming *SAVE ME* in my head over and over, but she only smiled and returned to her paperwork. "Let me tell you how it all goes," said the old man. "It goes like this: No matter what you believe, Life is eventually gonna come along and bend you over and have its way with you."

I gave him a disgusted look, but said nothing.

"That's what Life *does*, good sir. Life is *mean*, Life is *hard*, and it doesn't care what you believe in. When you least expect it, it'll come right on over to you and say, 'Bend over, bitch,' and it'll—"

"I get it," I said, rubbing my temples.

"That's where God comes in," the old man went on, undeterred by my obvious disinterest. "See, God's not gonna *stop* Life from having its way with you. No, good sir, that's not how God works. But what God *will* do, if you have accepted Him into your heart, is He'll hold your hand while Life is tagging you from the be-hind. God might even stroke your hair, if you're real tight with Him. And if the two of you are *super* close, and you're just a little bit lucky, God might even slip you some KY."

One of the techs entered the waiting room, looked at his clipboard, and said, "Seward?"

"That's me," I said to the old man, rising slowly to my feet, never so relieved to get irradiated.

The old man grabbed my wrist with his claw-like hand. "Listen to me, good sir. When the going gets rough, let me tell you—you'll be real grateful for that KY."

I looked down at him. "Can I tell *you* something?" I whispered.

"Yes, sir, you most certainly ca—"

"Fuck your God."

• • •

Lying on the cold, hard table, I watched the giant lens rotate around my head, listening to its low, whirring whine. That awful taste—sour and metallic—filled my mouth.

If there is a God, I thought, staring into the huge round lens, *that's what it looks like—God is a big, mechanical eye that shoots poison into its children.*

I lay there, feeling the poison enter me—tasting it, smelling it—and I did not pray.

TWENTY–SEVEN

IN THE PINES

I wake late the next morning, lying on the bathroom floor, to the sound of my phone ringing. The smell of puke rises from the toilet. A cockroach sits inches from my face, staring at me with indifference. My head feels like it's wrapped in Velcro leg weights.

My phone keeps ringing.

Beatrice.

Her name is like a gunshot in my head. I sit up too quickly, striking my head on the bottom of the sink. I curse and cry out, stumbling from the bathroom, lurching for my phone, which is lying face-down on the futon. I grab it, and the split-second it takes to turn it over stretches for what must be entire minutes.

UNCLE ARTHUR, reads the contact name on the screen.

I collapse onto the futon, feeling the anticipatory adrenaline rush out of me, leaving me cold and shivering. I could ignore him, but he'll keep calling. I swipe the screen and lift it dejectedly to my ear.

"Christ, took you long enough," grumbles Arthur. "Long night?"

"Something like that," I mumble, lighting a cigarette. The first drag brings a fresh wave of nausea, but the second one is a little better.

Arthur chuckles. "Yeah, mine was, too, but I suspect I had a better time than you did, judging from the sound of your voice."

I suck hard on my cigarette, my eyes squeezed shut, and don't say anything.

"Listen, I need a favor, yeah?"

I don't tell him to take his favor and shove it. I don't tell him I'm hung over and hung up on a fifteen-year-old girl and want to be left alone. I don't tell him I want to die. I tell him, "Sure, name it."

"We're changing the location of tonight's party from the Sunset Marquis to The Standard—the West Hollywood one, not the downtown one. I need you to call everyone on the guestlist and let them know. Also, the catering company. And . . . I can't remember if we did floral arrangements for this one, but if we did, call the florist, too, yeah? I've already emailed you the guestlist."

I'd forgotten about tonight's party. Arthur sold his propane company last week to an overseas buyer for a huge profit. He hasn't shut up about it. "Okay," I croak. "I'll take care of it."

"Man, you sound like shit. What did you do last night?"

I look over at the toilet. The stench wafting from it is almost visible. "I . . . don't remember," I say.

"Well, I hope it wasn't anything I wouldn't do." He snickers. "Aren't you going to ask what *I* did last night?"

I don't tell him I don't give a shit what he did last night. I don't tell him his life isn't as interesting as he thinks it is. I tell him flatly, "What did you do last night, Uncle Arthur."

He snickers again. He can't even help himself. "Let's just say there's a girl I haven't been able to get out of my mind. Let's just say there's a certain pizza-themed shoot we did with this girl that I've been watching pretty much every night for the last couple of months. Let's just say *she's* what I did."

The phone falls from my hand.

A crimson rage descends upon me, blotting out my vision. My blood ignites into bubbling magma. My lungs burn with each belabored breath. The words *I'LL KILL HIM* appear before my eyes in fiery red letters. *I'LL KILL HIM. I'LL KILL HIM. I'LL KILL HIM.*

When I lift the phone back to my ear with a trembling hand, he's still prattling on. "—a new indie movie she'd be perfect for, and, of course, there *is* no indie movie, but *she* doesn't know that. We spent all day and all night together, and Ty, let me tell you, it was heaven on fucking earth. That girl . . . god*damn*, that *girl*." He whistles. "Fucks like an A-list porn star, I'm not even shitting you. If I hadn't had her blood on my dick that first time, I wouldn't believe she'd been a virgin." He pauses, considering something. "Then again, it's been a couple of months since we last boned, so . . . who knows? Maybe she's gotten some more experience. She *did* have some new moves. Christ, Ty, I've got half a mind to drum up a *real* movie for her to star in." He laughs. "I won't, of course, but I've half a mind to."

I'LL KILL HIM. I'LL KILL HIM.

"Anyway, make those calls, yeah? I'll see you tonight." He clicks off.

I spend the next hour sobbing into my pillow, occasionally punching the floor and biting my arm. I can't quite figure out why I'm reacting like this. He's fucked her before. It's not like she and I are an . . . item. I don't, necessarily, have any right to be upset.

And yet . . . I am, and horribly so. I guess I'd thought there was something between us, something unspoken but understood. I had laid myself bare before her, shown her my most guarded, innermost self. And, on top of that, I *like* her. I like her quite a great deal. When, before her, was the last time I even had a simple conversation with another human being for the sake of the conversation, and not because I was trying to get something out of them?

I'm using you to feel better. The same way you're using me to feel better.

She had acknowledged that herself, so if it was true, how is she supposed to make me feel better if she's going to fuck my uncle every time he waves a bogus career opportunity in front of her face?

I want to text her horrible things. I want to call her and scream into the phone; scream so loud she *feels* my pain. I want to shout *WHY?* at her over and over until she breaks down and begins to weep. I want to do all of these things, but I will do none of them. All I will do is pull myself together, open my email, and start calling rich people to tell them their stupid party has changed locations.

I'm picking up my phone when it begins to ring. It's Beatrice.

After a brief moment of deliberation, I hit "Ignore."

TWENTY–EIGHT

LOOSE LIPS

BEHIND the front desk in the lobby of The Standard, there's a glass box built into the wall with a girl inside of it. The girl is maybe twenty-two, twenty-three, naked except for matching red-and-white polka-dotted bra and underwear, lying on her stomach and sucking on a lollipop, looking bored while she scrolls something–probably Instagram–on her phone.

For the first few minutes upon my arrival at the hotel, I can only stand there, looking at her, wondering how someone ends up with a job like that. I wonder what she gets paid, or if she's getting paid at all.

Aside from my still-smoldering rage toward Arthur and my despondent, crushing despair over Beatrice's betrayal, I'm feeling pretty okay because I didn't have to deal with the stress of finding parking; I'd decided to take a Lyft here because I had a pretty decent parking space near my apartment I didn't want to give up, and the sixteen-dollar ride (no tip–the driver had been blaring hardcore hip-hop and his air-conditioning was broken) had been worth it. I'd also only spent about forty-five minutes getting ready, as opposed to the usual hour, because I couldn't be bothered to give as much of a shit as I usually do. The moderate respite from my vanity is, to my surprise, kind of refreshing.

I make my way to the pool area, where the party is happening. Rich people stand around looking bored, staring blankly at whatever is on their phones–probably Instagram. I fake-smile and shake hands with a couple of businessmen who pretend to recognize me because they assume I'm Somebody Important, most likely because of the suit I'm wearing. After taking a glass of gin–seventy-three calories; not a huge deal–from a passing waitress in a miniskirt and bikini top, I walk over to where Arthur and Aunt Carlotta are standing by the glass wall that looks out at the city. Arthur is talking to some fat guy in Bermuda shorts and a Hawaiian shirt.

"Ty," Arthur says warmly upon my approach. His eyes are glassy, the muscles in his face loose; he's already drunk. "Nice to see you've made it out into the land of the living, though I must say you're still looking a bit green." He chuckles to himself and nods at my gin, "Ah, well, nothing like the hair of the dog that bit you to ease the pain, yeah?" He grins and raises his flute of champagne to me. I clink it, looking at the glass wall behind him and wondering how hard I'd have to push him in order to break it and send him tumbling down the hill, hopefully to his demise.

"Nothing like it," I say, forcing a smile I know must make me look deranged because Arthur recoils slightly.

"Tyler, honey, we're so glad you could make it," Aunt Carlotta says, as if I'd had some sort of choice in the matter. She smiles and squeezes my arm, and I notice she is, in fact, smoking an L&M. I think of Beatrice, and it takes everything in me not to break my glass over Arthur's head.

"We certainly *are*," says the fat guy in the Hawaiian shirt. His voice is what you'd imagine a Big Mac would sound like if it could talk. "It's been much too long." He bats his eyes at me, looking me up and down.

I swallow, trying not to let my face betray my disgust. I clear my throat and say, "Um. Have we . . . met?"

"Oh, sweetie, you remember Norm," says Aunt Carlotta. There's something odd about her face when she says this, and her tone of voice seems more unnatural than usual, but all I can do is assume she's tipsy. "You met him when you visited us that summer, when you were just a boy."

She's referring to the first time I came to Los Angeles. I'd been ten, I think, and my mom had raised the idea of my spending a few weeks of summer vacation with her rich brother and sister-in-law, to see how I liked it. I remembered trips to Disneyland, following Arthur around high-rise offices in Century City, movies with Aunt Carlotta at the Arclight, being introduced to a handful of celebrities—but nothing about this Norm fellow.

"Yes," says the fat man, "the last time I saw you, you were just a wee lad. Cute as a button, too. You've grown into quite a strapping young man, if you don't mind my saying so." I do mind his saying so. "A bit too skinny, but a tasty morsel, nonetheless."

"Uh, thanks," I say, sipping my gin.

"Norm here was an integral part in securing the deal to sell United Propane," says Arthur, clapping Norm on the shoulder. "He's spent the last three months in Europe, ferreting out the moolah."

With a greasy, booming laugh, Norm says, "Wish I could say it was all work and no play, but . . ." He shrugs, laughing again. "Those boys in Amsterdam . . ." He whistles through his teeth, shaking his head and grinning. "I'll tell ya, they don't make 'em like that here in the States." With an appreciative glance at me, he adds, "Although, *you*, my boy, would make out like a *bandit* over there."

"I'll . . . um . . . keep that in mind." I clear my throat again. "Listen," I say to Arthur, "I have to make . . . a phone call."

Arthur takes a long sip of his champagne, tottering on his feet. "Nonsense, stay and chat, yeah? Allison will be all right." He winks.

"She's not—Wait, what?" I say, taken aback, trying to remember if I've ever mentioned Allison to him. I'm almost certain I haven't. I keep my private life closely guarded from Arthur's watchful eye, and besides, the whole reason I'm with her is because her father is Plan B if Arthur's myriad connections don't end up working out for me, so I have no reason to inform him of her existence.

"Couples fight, it's normal," Arthur says, smiling sloppily at me and shrugging. He sways again. "Just apologize to her later. She'll get over it. But right now, you're here to have fun, yeah?"

"Apologize . . . for what?" I whisper, my stricken voice barely audible.

Arthur must not hear me because he turns to Aunt Carlotta and says, "Dearest, be a doll and get me another champagne, yeah?"

"I think you've had enough, darling."

"Enough?" Arthur laughs boisterously. "The night's just *begun*! Fine, I'll get it myself." He saunters off, nearly tripping twice over his own feet.

Distracted, my head spinning, I walk away in the other direction, not even sure where I'm going. I'm only *almost* certain I've never mentioned Allison; there's a chance her name might have slipped out at one point or another, though I doubt it. But our argument? I'm *one hundred percent positive* I never said anything about that to anyone, much less Arthur, and the only way he could—

My thoughts are interrupted by the feeling of a hand on my arm. I spin around, and Norm's big, sweating face is inches from mine. His rotund belly presses against my tie. "You know," he says, pelting my face with acrid, alcoholic breath. "I've got a room here. A *suite*, actually." He leans closer, pulling me to him, and whispers in my ear, "What do you say we dust off some old memories?"

I reel backward, spilling gin on my sport coat. "What did you say to me?" I say, my voice strained and raspy.

That booming laugh again, and Norm says with another wink, "Come find me if you change your mind." He twinkles his fingers at me and walks away.

I sit hard on the edge of one of the chaise lounges, nearly tipping it over. All around me, attractive people are talking and laughing, but I can't hear any of it. Some of them are dancing in place, so there must be music playing, but I can't hear that, either. All I can hear is, *What do you say we dust off some old memories?*

A coincidence, I tell myself. The only people who know about the feather duster are Beatrice and Judy. I *suppose* there's a slim chance Beatrice could have told Arthur about it when they were together yesterday, and he could have told Norm, but . . . no. There's no way. Beatrice wouldn't do that. She *couldn't*. And even if she *could*, that would mean Arthur knows about her and me, and I'd have been able to tell if that was the case.

No, Arthur doesn't know anything about me and Beatrice. But . . .

He *does* know about Allison.

And the only possible way he could know about Allison—

She doesn't need anything from you.

Everyone has an angle.

I pull out my phone and text Allison: *Are you home?* I wait for the response, clutching my phone with shaking, sweating hands. I notice a guy with a blond crewcut standing by himself, holding a seemingly untouched martini and staring at me. He looks sort of familiar, but I can't place him. I glare at him until he looks away. My phone vibrates: *yea*, is Allison's response.

Is your dad home?

After another few minutes, Allison replies, *is he ever?*

I'm coming over, I text. And, breaking my double-text rule for the second time in twenty-four hours, I add, *We need to talk*.

TWENTY-NINE

THE ANGLE

I kind of black out on the ride to Allison's house; one minute I'm getting into a Lyft, the next I'm standing in the doorway of Allison's huge bedroom, my fists clenched, my breathing heavy. She's sitting on her couch wearing a short tank top and panties, no makeup, her legs crossed, staring at her phone. It takes her a few moments to realize I'm standing there. When she finally looks up at me, she asks, "Did you come to apologize?" She looks me over, taking in my demeanor, and adds, "You don't *look* like you came to apologize."

Just apologize to her later. Arthur's voice in my ears, like he's standing right behind me. *She'll get over it.*

"Why did you approach me at that party." It isn't a question. I've got her all figured out. "That night, when we first met—why did you approach me."

She cocks her head, re-crosses her legs, bouncing her foot. "What

167

are you talking about?" she asks, and it's a shame she doesn't have acting aspirations because she'd fucking kill it.

"You know what I'm talking about. The night we met. *You* approached *me*. Why?"

She shrugs, looks back down at her phone. "I don't know, you're hot." She shrugs again. "There was no one else there I wanted to bang."

I storm over to her and knock her phone out of her hands. I'd hoped it would smash against the wall, but it lands with a soft thud on the plush carpet.

"*Whoa*," Allison says. "You need to—"

"I don't *need* to do *anything*. *You* need to start fucking talking."

She stands, getting in my face. "Listen, asshole, I don't know who the fuck you think you—"

"How does my uncle know about us? What did you tell him?"

Her face softens into an expression of complete surprise, and I'm certain it's real. "Wait," she says, "he told you?"

"*TOLD ME WHAT*?" I bellow into her face, making her flinch.

She sits back down on the couch, tucking her legs beneath her, and sighs. "Okay," she says evenly, "what *exactly* did he tell you?"

I can feel the blood rushing into my face, pushed there by a furiously pumping heart. My vision blurs. "It does not fucking matter what he told me. I want to hear it from you."

She sighs again, and then she actually starts examining her fingernails. "Look," she says. "Really, I was just a backup. I was only there to fill in whatever blanks his other people missed."

168

"His . . . other people?"

"Yeah. I mean, you know. The people he has following you. Didn't he tell you about that?"

The burning rage flushes out of me, replaced by an icy, all-consuming chill.

The black Accord. The guy with the blond crewcut.

"Shit," says Allison, seeing it in my face. "Fuck. Listen, I didn't have anything to do with that part of it, okay? He told me about it when we worked out the arrangement. What I do—it's not even that big of a deal. You tell me things, and I relay them back to Arthur." She pauses. "The main thing was the script, but I never got, like, *why*, you know? Don't take this the wrong way, or anything, but . . . I mean, *seriously*, *no* one is going to make that thing. So, like, I never got why he was so worried about killing it every time you managed to get it in the hands of some nobody."

I have to sit down. I can't take this. I step slowly backward, not seeing anything, and sit on the edge of her bed.

"I mean, has he even *read* it? Because, like, *I* have, and . . . well, come on. You *have* to know it's not going anywhere."

He hasn't read it. He never reads scripts, and mine is no different. For all he knows, it could have all the potential for a blockbuster smash-hit. And if *that* happened, I'd be out from under his thumb. I feel sick, appalled at myself for not seeing it sooner.

I'LL KILL HIM. I'LL KILL HIM. I'LL KILL HIM.

The room is silent for a while. I concentrate on my breathing, feeling each breath go in and out, doing what I can to keep it steady. When I raise my eyes and look at Allison, she's retrieved her phone from the floor and is once again absorbed in whatever's on the screen. Probably Instagram. "There's one thing I don't get," I say.

Looking up from the phone, she asks, "What don't you get? I explained everything, just like you wanted."

"Why?" I ask. "Why did you do it? For eight months, you've strung me along, and for . . . what? What did you get out if it?"

She shrugs. "I was bored."

"You were . . . *bored?*"

"Yeah. I mean, he offered me money, but, like . . ." she gestures around at the enormous bedroom ". . . what do I need money for? I have more than I could ever spend. So, then he offered me a part in some TV show, but *honestly*—me, an actress?" She laughs. "No way in *hell*. I'd rather fuck myself with a chainsaw."

I'm trying to think if I know anyone who owns a chainsaw.

"I don't know what you're so bent out of shape about," Allison goes on, returning to her phone. "I mean, come on, what did you *think* this was? I have everything I want. I can have any *guy* I want." She glances at me, but only briefly. "Like, sure, you're hot, or whatever, but there are lots of hot guys. And lots of them aren't twenty-eight-year-old assistants who live in shitty little starter apartments in Hollywood."

"Stop," I say quietly.

"To be honest, I'm kind of glad the gig is up. It was fun for the first few months. It was, like, *exciting*. But then . . ." She trails off, shrugging again. Always with the fucking shrugging. "But then it was just another thing to do."

"Stop," I repeat. It sounds pained, pleading, and I hate myself for it.

"Really, it's your own fault for not figuring it out sooner. All that interest I took in your life? Your life isn't that interesting. *You're* not that interesting. You *think* you are, which I guess is why you would prattle on about all the mundane details of your day and assume I gave a shit. God, I can't tell you how *hard* it was to pretend with you, sometimes. It would be one thing if the sex was at least good, but . . ." Shrug. "I mean, look, chill. I've had way worse."

I'm getting to my feet. I'm walking toward her.

"And, hey, for what's it worth, you're not, like, the *worst* writer. I showed my dad your script, and he said *he* wouldn't give it to anyone, but he definitely knows of people in this town who would buy it. He says you wouldn't get *much* for it, and, of course, it would never end up getting *made*, but you'd get *something*. So, like, don't give up, you know?"

I'm standing over her.

"Then again," she says, "maybe you should. Give up, I mean. There's no shame in knowing something is never gonna happen. There's nothing wrong with cutting your losses. You're still young. Well, *sort* of. Not *here*, you're not, but somewhere else, like back in Bishop." She says "Bishop" as though it tastes sour. "In Bishop, you'd still be young. You could go back there and have your whole life ahead of you." She looks up from her phone and seems surprised to see me standing there, but then her lips curl into a cruel smile, her braces glinting. She glares into my eyes and says, "Hollywood isn't for every-one."

THIRTY

THE MACHINE

LEAVING Allison's house, massaging my bleeding knuckles with a paper towel and trying to figure out how I'm going to kill Arthur, I walk to the end of the street and hail a Lyft. When it arrives, I tuck the bloody paper towel into the inside pocket of my jacket and climb in back. I take out my phone and see I have two text messages from Beatrice: *what r u doing?* and *r u ok?* I stare at the screen, my thumbs hovering over the keyboard, unable to decide if I should say something nasty to her. Because of my preoccupation, I don't immediately notice the driver is grinning at me in the rearview mirror. It's only when I realize we're not moving that I look up.

My phone falls from my hands, tumbling onto the floor of the car.

"You never called me."

I'm about to get right back out of the car, but the driver throws it in gear and guns forward. The doors lock with a panic-inducing *thunk*.

My mind flashes to the "parking ticket" this guy had given me back in June, which is now buried in my junk drawer; I hadn't been able to make myself throw it away because I was afraid doing so would invite a host of bad omens, or something.

"You're . . . a Lyft driver now?" is all I can come up with to say.

The guy shrugs, looking at me in the rearview mirror—from which, I notice, hangs a Jesus fish and a metal crucifix. I can tell he's smiling from the way his creepy eyes crinkle at the edges, but I can't see his mouth. Remembering the way his grin had eaten up most of his face, I'm glad for that. "I wear a lot of hats," he explains. "I suppose you *could* say that I do a little bit of everything. How's Beatrice doing?"

Gripping my knees with sweating hands, I ask, "How do you know her name?"

He titters, and it's like the scrape of dead leaves over an uneven side-walk. "*Doing* a little bit of everything comes with *knowing* a little bit of everything," he says. "Except calculus, of course. Never quite did get the hang of that." He looks at me in the mirror again, his black irises blazing in the light of the passing streetlamps. "You've got it pretty bad for her, huh?" He tsks and shakes his head, sighing. "Few things are better than falling in love. Fewer things are worse."

"I'm not in love with her," I say defensively. My mind flashes on a phantom image of her with Arthur in his gargantuan water bed, making me want to throw up. I rub my temples and shut my eyes, unable to come to rational grips with the situation. "Who the fuck *are* you?" I ask, hating how helpless and frightened I sound.

Ignoring my question, the guy says, "No, I guess 'love' isn't *exactly* the right word, is it, now? I know that your little girlfriend—the cheer-leader, sorry, not Beatrice, and I'm *guessing* from the blood on your hands that she's your *ex*-girlfriend now, but I digress—anyway, I know she suggested you can't love anyone but yourself, but *that's* not totally true, either, am I right? I mean, she's on to *something*, but she's over-shot it *just* a *bit*. You're *obsessed* with yourself, yes, but you don't *love* yourself. You *can't* because you *hate* yourself, deep down. That's why you can't eat like a normal human being. That's why you torture those girls. You hate yourself."

"Wait a second," I say. "I never 'tortured' anyone. All of them con-sented."

He titters again, making my already-clammy skin break out in goose-flesh. "Yes, well," he says, "*consent* is a bit of a sticky subject nowadays, isn't it? It doesn't exactly *mean* what it *used* to."

"Whatever. I haven't done it in . . . a while."

He waves his freakishly long-fingered hand. "Yes, yes, of course. I suppose beating up sixteen-year-olds doesn't *count*, but regardless, we're getting off-topic. The point I was getting at is, while maybe you don't *love* sweet little Beatrice, you're definitely obsessed with her. Which, I *suppose*, is probably the closest *you* can *get* to love."

"That's bullshit. What I had with Judy was . . . something. It was . . . close."

"Is that so? Tell me, what *precisely* did you like about her?"

I'm dismayed that I have to think about it for a second. "I liked how she . . . made me feel, I guess. And I liked how she . . . looked." I shake

175

my head, disgusted with myself—*why* am I explaining myself to this freak?

"That is *precious*. And to answer your unspoken question—it's because you know I'm the real deal. What you're feeling right now—that's the logical part of your brain at odds with what you know to be true. This is happening. This is real. *I* am real."

I swallow, my mouth dry and sticky. My body is enveloped in a sheen of hot sweat. My clothes are dampening. "Where are you . . . taking me?" I ask pitifully.

The guy glances at the GPS on his dashboard-mounted iPhone. "Five-eight-four-nine Sunset Boulevard—that's home, right? Cool it, man, I'm taking you where you want to go. We're talking, that's all." He takes a pack of Dunhills out of his center console and puts one in his mouth. "You don't mind if I smoke, do you?" he asks. "You're not going to give me a one-star rating, or anything like that?" I don't say anything, so he shrugs and lights the cigarette with a snap of his fingers—which is honestly the least surprising thing he's done thus far. "Anyway," he goes on, "we have to talk about Beatrice, because your *little* obsession is going to turn into a *big* problem, and quite soon."

"If you're threatening me . . . If you're going to go to the cops, or something . . ."

"Oh, *please*, do I *look* like the kind of guy who gives a shit about who fucks whom?" He glances at the fish and the crucifix hanging from the mirror and laughs a little. Gesturing at the ornaments, he says, "Ah, don't mind *those*. Those are just for show. Listen, spoiler alert—I don't give *half* of a low-flying fuck about the whole age thing. I do, however, care about *you*, in a manner of speaking, and *you* are about to find yourself in a rather sticky spot of trouble."

"Why do you care about me? *Who the fuck* are *you?*"

"You're a very integral part of a much bigger machine," he says. "I have a vested interest in the *continuation* of that machine's operation, and I have to be sure you don't break it."

Something occurs to me. "Wait," I say. "Are you . . . *hitting* on me?"

He glares at me in the mirror. "Come on, man, you're smarter than that. There are people from whom I'd expect questions like that, but you *know* better."

I don't, actually, but for some reason I decide no, that's not what this is, he's not hitting on me. "What machine are you talking about, then? What are you afraid I'm going to . . . break?"

"Look, you've got some things to figure out," the guy says, starting to sound impatient. "I'd rather hoped you'd have connected the dots by now, but there's still time. Not *much* time, but *some* time. You're going to have to make a decision, and it's of vital importance to me that you make the *right* decision. I can't spell it out for you because, frankly, that's not my style. But I *can* point you in the right direction."

"I have no idea what you're talking about."

The guy rolls his window down and blows out a long stream of smoke. "No," he says, "I know you don't. Listen, here's as much as I'm willing and able to tell you—like I said, you're going to have to make a choice. There will be *three* possible outcomes when said choice presents itself. For simplicity's sake, let's call them *A*, *B*, and *C*. Now, here's the fun part—you can pick *B* or *C*, and everything will be fine. It doesn't matter which. Both *B* and *C* are perfectly acceptable. Option *A*, on the other hand . . . well, let's just say that would be a *colossal* clusterfuck for all parties involved. Yourself included, but *me*, more importantly."

"Okay," I say, stretching the word out, still unable to fully acknowledge to myself that I'm even entertaining this fucker's nonsense. "What's Option *A*, and why can't I . . . choose it?"

"Don't get too hung up on the specifics, man, it's not that complicated. It's all pretty straightforward. All you need to know is that *A* is strictly a no-go. Do not collect two hundred dollars, and so on, and so forth."

"Um . . . huh?"

He eyes me in the mirror and gives a brusque shake of his head. "Christ, you kids. Look, I can give you *one* hint, one little *nudge*, but that's it, *comprende*? Don't ask for any more than that because I'm already indulging your ignorance *way* too much. At some point, the training wheels have to come off, you get me?"

"Yeah, I . . . get you."

"Then listen up." He stops at a red light where Highland intersects Sunset, and he turns around. His face is cold and grim and terrifying. His onyx eyes smolder as they stare into mine, and it feels like my eyeballs are cooking in their sockets, but I can't look away. "What you have to figure out," he says, "once and for all, is the yellow woman. Once you
178

figure out the yellow woman, everything else will just . . . *click* right into place."

What do you say we dust off some old memories?

The guy grins, and it's a normal grin, amiable and warm. It would be comforting if it wasn't for the words which had preceded it.

"What do you know about her?" I ask. The sweat on my body has become ice-cold.

"Man, I know *all* about her," the guy says, his grin stretching. Not quite to the superhuman width I'd seen the night he'd given me the fake ticket, but enough to be unsettling. "Unfortunately, *you* don't seem to know *shit* about her, and you need to ameliorate that *right* quick." He turns around, and the light becomes green. The car jets forward, and I dash perspiration from my forehead with the cuff of my sleeve.

"If I figure her out," I say, "whatever that even means, will I be able to stop her from coming?"

"You're not paying at*ten*tion," the guy says, annoyance creeping into his voice. "If you figure her out, you won't *have* to stop her." He winks at me in the rearview mirror. It's a cruel wink, jeering and antagonistic.

When we arrive, he swerves into the Mobil station next to my building because he'd have to make an illegal U-turn to pull up along the curb out front. He parks in front of one of the gas pumps and turns around again. "Don't let me down, kid," he says. "I've got a lot riding on you."

I give him a puzzled look, wondering again if he's hitting on me, and then I get out of the car without answering. I take a few paces toward my apartment building before wheeling around to get one last look at him. I hadn't even paid attention to what kind of car he was driving. When I turn around, though, all the pumps are unoccupied, and the only other person in the immediate vicinity is a homeless guy standing in the alley between the gas station and my building, smoking a cigarette in the shadows by the Dumpster. For a moment, I consider beating the shit out of him because no one is around and it's been a while since I've indulged in that particular hobby, but it seems like more energy than it's worth, so he gets a reprieve of which he'll never even be aware.

He smiles at me, waving. I don't wave back.

• • •

Inside my apartment, I stand before the closet, peering into the darkness and listening to the yellow woman's sickly breathing coming from the shadows. I'm holding my new feather duster.

What do you say we dust off some old memories?

My lips soundlessly form the words, and doing so has a kind of incantational effect, conjuring a swirl of unfocused, disconnected images. I can feel my brain trying to snuff them, to smother them, to keep them in the dark where they've lived in secret for so long, but for the first time, I fight it. I push back against the instinctive impulse to stuff it all down, envisioning an arm reaching into a hole and grasping at a dirty, long-buried photo album of old Polaroids. I imagine myself lifting the photo album from the earth, laying it on the ground before me, and—

The yellow woman hisses. I can barely make out the outlines of her saggy features. The stale smell of old cigarettes assaults my sinuses. "No," I tell her, the firmness in my voice at odds with the terror within me. "No. I need to see." I flick the light switch on the wall, casting a curtain of blackness over my apartment. The yellow woman needs no more invitation. She emerges from the closet on all fours before rising to her feet. She towers nearly a foot above me. When she reaches her gnarled hand toward me, I take a step back and hold out the feather duster, presenting it to her like an offering—which, in a way, I suppose it sort of is.

"Show me," I tell her. Silent tears stream from my eyes. My mind reels and screams, frantic and distraught, begging to let it protect me from the things it's kept hidden for so long. I am cold, shivering uncontrollably. "I need to see," I say again. "Show me what I need to see."

The yellow woman's rubbery lips stretch into a ghastly grin, and she takes the feather duster from me, running her long, pale tongue over its handle, sucking and slobbering on it as though she were performing sloppy fellatio. Her phlegmy saliva drips in fat globs from the white plastic.

Lubrication, I think to myself. *She's lubricating it.*

I unbutton my pants, letting them fall to the floor. Kicking them aside, I turn around, my back to the yellow woman, and get on my hands and knees, presenting her with what she wants. What she's always wanted. "Show me," I say, and she does.

THIRTY-ONE

THE YELLOW WOMAN

I am ten years old, and it is summer. I've been in Los Angeles for a little over a week, mostly having a good time, doing things a child would enjoy doing.

All of that is about to end.

I don't know it yet, but childhood is over.

I am sitting at the dining room table, eating a sandwich. It is the last time I will ever eat without feeling shame. Aunt Carlotta is sitting next to me, sipping a martini and smoking an L&M—this is back when Arthur still let her smoke in the house. Norm, a man she knows through some sort of work Uncle Arthur does, is sitting beside her. They are whispering to each other. I don't pay them a whole lot of attention. I am enjoying my sandwich.

"I *do* love those Frisk boys," Aunt Carlotta says, leaning back in her chair. "I just don't *know*. I mean, you must *understand*, Tyler is my *nephew*. How much did you say?" I look up at the mention of my name.

Norm's fat, sweaty face grins. He whispers something in Aunt Carlotta's ear. Aunt Carlotta whistles. "Things *have* been tighter than I'd like. Arthur is actually *monitoring* my *expenses*, if you can believe it. The IRS is apparently breathing down his neck about *something* or another. He even *shouted* at me last week when I bought a new Mercedes, but I *always* buy the new model as soon as it comes *out*."

Norm frowns, shaking his head sympathetically. "I won't breathe a word of the arrangement to Arthur, naturally," he says. "Just think, you'd have all that money to play with, and he'd be none the wiser."

Aunt Carlotta looks at me, sucking on her cigarette. To Norm, she says, "I just don't know *why* they couldn't ask me *themselves*."

Norm's huge shoulders make a kind of jerking motion I guess is supposed to be a shrug. "I think they're embarrassed, is all. You understand. It's a bit of a precarious request."

"Yes, but if they're offering *that* kind of money . . ." She sips her drink and looks at me again, her brow furrowed. "Tyler, sweetie, how would you like to spend some time with those nice singers you met at the party the other night?" She studies me and asks, "You do like Frisk's music, don't you?"

"Not really," I say, a little too quickly. All the girls in school love Frisk, but I think they're corny. Sensing this isn't the right response, I say, "I mean, they're okay, I guess." I shrug. "They seemed . . . nice." Actually, they'd seemed creepy, in a way I couldn't figure out, but I didn't want to be rude.

"Wait until you see their condo," says Norm. "Best view in the city, if I'm to be perfectly honest."

"We would have to . . . prepare him," says Aunt Carlotta to Norm. "Don't you think? We can't just ship him off without him knowing what to . . . expect."

Norm licks his lips. Something about it makes me lose my appetite, and I put my sandwich down, pushing my plate away. "I'll prepare him, if you'd like," he says. "I'll show him *exactly* what to expect."

"Oh, Norm, *stop* that," laughs Aunt Carlotta, playfully smacking Norm's meaty arm. Her cheeks are flushed. "But . . . I *do* have an idea."

• • •

"You want me to . . . take my clothes off?" I ask uneasily, shifting my wide-eyed gaze between Aunt Carlotta and Norm. We're standing in the living room. Aunt Carlotta is holding a feather duster she's retrieved from the maid's supply closet.

Aunt Carlotta bites her lip, fingering the handle of the feather duster. "You see," she says, "the Frisk boys are going to . . . Well, what they're going to do is—"

"They're going to play a game with you," Norm cuts in. He's perspiring profusely. Sweat drips off his nose and makes little dots on his bright blue button-down shirt. "It's a very fun game. It's the best game. But you have to be naked in order to play."

"Yes, that's right," says Aunt Carlotta, brightening. "A *game*. A *secret* game. You can't tell anyone about this game. Not even your parents." She pauses, thinking, pursing her lips. "*Especially* not your parents."

"What happens if I tell?" I ask.

"Well," says Aunt Carlotta, frowning. "You'll, um . . . You'll have to—"

"You'll die," says Norm.

"Oh, *Norm*, don't *scare* him." She says this, but she's grinning.

"He has the right to know." Norm gets on his knee, an action that clearly pains him. He looks into my face. I can smell meat and cheese, and something starchy, like laundry detergent. "If you tell anyone, you'll die," he says. "A horrible woman will come out of your closet and she'll eat you while you're sleeping."

"Oh, Norm, for *God's* sake," says Aunt Carlotta, but there's something in her face that doesn't match her irritated words and tone of voice. It's something like . . . excitement. She lights a cigarette and begins fanning her face with the feather duster.

"I don't think I want to play this game," I say.

"Sure you do," says Norm, pulling my shirt over my head. His fingers are warm and wet when they graze my skin. "You're going to have so much fun." He unbuttons my shorts and tugs them down. My underwear follows. "Now, what you're going to want to do—" he's starting to wheeze "—is turn around . . . and bend over."

Aunt Carlotta walks over to us, pursued by her cloud of cigarette smoke. The excitement in her face is unmistakable. The smell of stale tobacco wafts off her. She kneels in front of me, beside Norm, and strokes my face. "Now, Tyler, darling," she says. "There's nothing to fear. I'm just going to show you how to play."

And she does.

• • •

That night, I'm sitting alone in the master bathroom of the guest house, shivering in front of the toilet. I've just vomited for the fourth time in the last hour. I keep thinking of how cold and hard the handle of the feather duster had been when Aunt Carlotta slid it inside me. Of how big and pink Norm's penis had been when he'd started touching it. Of how hot the white stuff had been when it had splashed onto my face.

I don't like the game at all, but I've already played it, and if I tell anyone, something horrible is going to come for me. I'd thought I was too old to believe in that kind of thing, but when Norm had said it, I knew he was telling the truth. It had been something in his eyes.

I hurl myself upon the toilet and throw up again.

• • •

The next morning, the triplets pick me up from the compound and take me back to their penthouse condo in West Hollywood.

For most of the first day, they're extra nice to me. They keep giving me ice cream and candy I don't want. They let me watch R-rated movies

Les goes first. He takes a long time. Lex goes next, but he doesn't take as long. Len goes last, and he takes the longest.

Next, they take the dental device out of my mouth and make me suck on their penises—sometimes one at a time, sometimes two at a time, and sometimes all three get crammed in at once. Les shoots his white stuff into my mouth, and when I gag and try to spit it out, he scoops it off my chin and forces it back into my mouth, saying, "Be a good whore, babesy, and *swallow.*"

When that's over, they leave me alone for a little while and start doing things to each other on the floor—touching each other, sucking on each other, putting things inside each other, *et cetera.* Then, they disappear, leaving me tied up, sobbing, screaming for my mother. I eventually fall asleep, but my dreams are a hallucinatory montage of the day's events, so there is no relief.

• • •

The second day is the same.

• • •

By dawn of the third day, I am old, I am tired, and I am broken.

It is also on the third day the triplets decide they need to add more boys to the mix.

"He's just *too* cute," Les complains to the other two after they've each had a turn with me. "I want to ruin him. Like, really, *really* fuck him up. If we don't get someone here whom I can actually hurt, I'm going to hurt *him*."

"I want to kill him," Len says in his robotic monotone. He stares at me with glassy eyes. "I want to cut him open and play around with his blood."

Lex wags his finger at them. "That would explicitly violate Carlotta's rules. If he has a scratch on him when we bring him back . . ."

Les rolls his eyes. "I know, I *know*, you keep re*minding* me. Let's hurry up and get someone expendable over here, *stat*, or I'm going to say to *hell* with Lottie's silly rules." He grins at me.

Lex gets out his cell phone and starts making some calls.

By that afternoon, three additional boys have been procured. They're older than I am by a few years. One is Mexican, one is black, and the other is Asian. Les whines about this, saying he'd wanted blonds. Lex tells him it's the best he could get on short-notice. "Besides," he says, "minorities are always cheaper."

There's a soundproofed room with a heart-shaped bed and all kinds of medieval-looking sex equipment. While Lex had been making phone calls, Len and Les had made me help them cover everything in the room with clear plastic tarpaulin. When the new boys arrive, we all gather in the sex room. Things get underway pretty quickly. There are no pleasantries or façades. I wonder if the boys know they're going to die. Something in their downcast eyes tells me they do.

First, the triplets make the Asian boy do stuff to me while they fondle the other two. They keep issuing commands. "Eat his ass," they say through a mouthful of genitals. "Suck his cock. Great, now rim him. Fabulous. Stick a finger in his ass. Two fingers. Get your whole fucking fist up there."

When they get tired of this, they have the boys stand in a line so they can piss on them. "Come get in on this, babesy," Les tells me as he showers the Mexican kid's face with his urine.

"I don't have to go," I says.

"Then come lick it off."

By this point, I know it's best to do as I'm told.

I had thought it would be Les who would instigate the violence, but it ends up being Len. He's fucking the black boy on the bed, and after he pulls out and ejaculates onto his stomach, he starts slapping him. The slaps start light. They're almost playful. Len is giggling, and the boy starts giggling, too. But the slaps grow harder, and eventually turn into punches. Blow after blow rains down on the boy's face. Blood begins to dot the plastic sheet. The boy whimpers and turns his head to the side to spit out several dislodged teeth.

Les is rallied by Len's actions. He has his cock in the Asian boy's mouth. As Len is punching the black boy, Les hoots and backhands the Asian boy across the face. The boy falls onto his side, and Les leaps up and starts kicking him in the ribs and stomach. He's still wearing his shoes.

Lex is busy moving the barrel of a wooden baseball bat in and out of the Mexican boy's asshole. When he sees what Les is doing, he pulls the bat out and tosses it to him. Les catches it, licking a reddish-brown smear from the barrel, and the Asian boy blinks tearfully up at him and begs him not to hurt him anymore. Les doesn't listen. He starts whacking the Asian boy in the torso, until his chest is all sunken and caved in. The Asian boy lies there, twitching, telling Les to "Just kill me. Please just kill me." Les turns around and holds out the blood- and shit-stained bat, offering it to me. "Here you go, babesy," Les says. "Give him what he wants."

I take the bat and stand over the boy. His eyes are round and hopeless.

I look at Lex, who has somehow managed to beat the Mexican boy so badly his face is now a large, cavernous hole. Lex is squatting over the boy's head, chewing on a torn-off finger, and shitting directly into the hole.

I look back down at the Asian boy. "Please," he whispers. Blood is trickling from the corner of his mouth.

Once, when helping my mother carry the groceries inside, I dropped a cantaloupe and it splattered open on the driveway.

That's what the Asian boy's head looks like after I hit it five or six times with the bat.

Len has gotten a knife from somewhere and has cut open the black boy's stomach. He's shoveling mashed-up handfuls of innards into his mouth and chewing them with a look of ecstasy on his face.

I think that's around the time I pass out.

• • •

Exiting the memory is like jolting awake from a vivid nightmare. For a few moments, I'm consumed with terror, thinking I'm still there, still living it, but then reality sets in, and the relief is unquantifiable. Even though I'm bent over with a feather duster shoved up my ass, it's better than being . . . back *then*.

It's no matter I can't remember the rest of it. The remainder of my time with the triplets, going back to Carlotta and Arthur, anything else that might have occurred that summer—it's all incidental. I've reclaimed the necessary parts, for better or worse.

I reach behind me and pull out the feather duster, dropping it on the floor. It's when I stand that I hear it.

Breathing.

Behind me.

My heart sinks. The terror returns. "*No*," I whisper, my body breaking out in fresh chills. She's supposed to be gone. I thought she'd be gone. Now that I know what she is, she's supposed to be gone.

But when I turn around, she's still there, squatting on her haunches, her stringy hair hanging in her face. She's picked up the feather duster and is licking the handle again.

Seeing her there, however, does not produce within me the usual reaction. Instead of the soul-shattering horror I've come to expect whenever I see her, there's only a kind of grim, resigned disappointment. I sigh, sitting on the futon and watching her lick the feather duster clean. A profound sadness enters me, starting small and expanding like a rapidly inflating balloon. How trivial it all is. How boring. Everything about me, every aspect of my personality, is a direct result of something that happened to me when I was ten years old. Nothing about me is unique. I'm just another victim.

I want to be disgusted with myself. I want to be appalled at the notion I could be so delicate, so easily broken. I want to insist to myself the child in me is dead, I'm a *man*, I'm impervious to something as pathetic as *trauma*. But I'm not, and I know it too wholeheartedly to deny it. What's worse, I want to reach inside myself and find that child, so I can hold him and protect him and prevent the horrible people in his life from destroying him and turning him into whatever it is I've become. I want so badly to do this, but I know it's too late.

It's too late for me.

As the yellow woman watches with grinning pleasure, I bury my face in my hands and begin to sob.

THIRTY–TWO

FALLING APART

FOR the next few weeks, I exist in a perpetual state of delirious inebriation. I start taking the Ambien around the clock, and when I can't sleep any more, I have vivid hallucinations that should terrify me, but ultimately leave me feeling annoyed and exhausted. When the Ambien runs out, I begin gobbling everything in my cabinet—Xanax, Vicodin, Percocet, Valium, and even a few stray Dilaudid and a lone tablet of Demerol. The volume on everything gets turned down. Time has a habit of rapidly speeding up and slowing to an almost insufferable crawl. The yellow woman is always there now—darkness or no darkness—but even she is a minor nuisance.

I only leave my apartment to buy cigarettes, liquor, and coke—those three things, along with the pills, are pretty much all I've been consuming, so I don't have to worry about food, though there's one instance when I come out of a Xanax-induced blackout to find myself devouring

194

a cheeseburger, and I have to run to the toilet to puke up the toxic calories.

The alcohol and cigarettes aren't difficult, because there's a liquor store within walking distance from my apartment, but the coke proves to be occasionally tricky; my dealer is usually somewhat close by, but not always. One night, I have to meet him all the way in Redondo Beach, and afterward I spend hours driving aimlessly on the freeways, too high to pay attention to my GPS or to even have a general idea of where I am.

My phone keeps blowing up, mainly with texts from Arthur and Beatrice. Beatrice's texts have edged into frantic, hysterical panic, and are peppered with repeated punctuation marks and emojis. Arthur's are angrier, more hostile, accusing me of being a lazy piece of shit who doesn't want to work. At some point, he texts me a picture of Allison's bruised, bloodied face, captioned with *YOU HAVE NO IDEA WHAT I HAD TO DO TO MAKE THIS GO AWAY.*

After about a week of sending unanswered texts, both Arthur and Beatrice start calling periodically—I delete their voicemails without listening to them. I think Arthur starts sending his goons to my apartment to check on me because someone keeps banging on my apartment door every few days, but it could also be one of the hallucinations. Besides, I'm sure he's got someone watching the door to my building, and since I still have to occasionally go out to replenish my chemical fixes, he must know I'm still alive.

I've discovered a song called "Narcissus" by someone named Bunny Lowe, and it speaks to some essential part of me I can't exactly identify.

I've been playing it on repeat for I don't know how long. I've probably listened to it at least a few thousand times by now, so I should know the words, but every time I try to sing along, the words to "Ohio is for Lovers" by Hawthorne Heights come out, instead, which is strange because I don't even listen to Hawthorne Heights. The yellow woman finds this impossibly funny, and her hoarse cackling is obnoxious, so I stop trying to sing along.

Somewhere in the middle of what I think is my third week of isolation, I get a notification on my phone reminding me of my annual PET scan in three days. I have to stare at the reminder for about half an hour before my drug-addled brain is able to attach some sort of meaning to it, and it occurs to me I should, most likely, try and sober myself up in time for the appointment. I consider skipping it in favor of continuing my drug binge until I run out of money, but I decide against doing that; I need to sober up, anyway, because if I burn all my cash on drugs, I won't be able to execute my Dying Alone in the Sun plan if the cancer has, indeed, returned.

Over the next couple of days, I wean myself off the hardest of the drugs—most of the pills are gone, in any case—and I even smoke some weed (which I despise) to ease the transition. Once the worst of my stupor has lifted, I have enough wherewithal to get on my scale, and I'm pleased to find I've lost six pounds.

You have to take the small victories where you can get them.

THIRTY–THREE

SLIGHTED

CONGRATULATIONS, Tyler. Your PET scan was clear."

I'll never forget how Dr. Wong had smiled when she'd told me that. She was a prim and serious woman, and before then, I don't think I'd ever seen her show any expression. I didn't like seeing genuine joy in her face. There was something hot about her cold, disaffected demeanor, and I'd often fantasized about what kinds of things she'd let me make her do if we'd met under different circumstances. That smile, though—that smile was all wrong. It didn't fit my perception of her. There are few things more annoying than when people break out of the molds into which you force them. I want everyone to behave in accordance with my perception of the world.

I hadn't known how to take the information she was giving me, either. I'd been expecting her to tell me the radiation hadn't worked, the cancer had spread to my major organs, and I had three months to live.

Telling me I was clear did nothing to reinforce the tragic narrative I'd been weaving for myself.

"So . . . that's it?" I'd asked her. "I'm . . . cured?"

"Well," she said, still smiling that stupid, out-of-character smile. "You'll have to get tested in another three months. If that scan is clear, too, we'll do another one three months after that. Then, we'll go to every six months, then every year, and so on. Just to be safe. But right now, everything looks perfectly normal. I'd say you have cause to celebrate."

The night before, I'd stuck the tube of a beer bong up a nineteen-year-old's asshole and poured a gallon of vinegar into her rectum. That had been my way of celebrating what little time I thought I had left.

I kind of wish I could say I felt bad. I thought about all the girls I'd dehumanized and debased, all because I thought I was dying, because I wanted them to feel how I felt. I thought about all the money I'd blown on shitty coke and cheap liquor. All those cigarettes I'd smoked because who gives a shit about lung cancer when a different kind of cancer is going to kill you first?

Most people, I guess, would feel something akin to regret. At the very least, they'd realize the error of their ways and, having been granted a new lease on life, they'd solemnly vow to change.

Me, though?

I felt slighted, like Some Great Being had royally ripped me off. I was pissed. I remember thinking, *What the fuck am I supposed to do now?* I'd been gearing up to die, and now I was going to live. More than that,

I was going to keep eking out my miserable existence, broke and bored and subservient to a tyrannical, sadistic entertainment mogul. What a wasted shell of a life.

"Tyler?" Dr. Wong said, frowning a little. That was better. It was better when she frowned. At least one thing was right in the world. "You don't seem as pleased as I'd anticipated."

"I'm . . . very pleased," I managed to say. "I'm just . . . in shock."

I knew her smile was going to return as soon as the words were out, and she disappointed me by not disappointing. "That's normal," she said. "Give yourself a day to let it sink in. But after that—*enjoy* it, Tyler. Let yourself relax. You've won this round."

I always hated when people used the "fight" allegory when talking about dealing with cancer. You don't *fight* cancer; cancer kicks your ass. It wouldn't even be a fair fight, anyway. It's a ravenous, destructive disease that eats you from the inside out. All the bullshit about staying positive and adjusting your outlook doesn't mean shit when you're at odds with the most lethally effective ailment on the planet.

She asked me if I had any questions for her before she let me go, and I told her no, I didn't.

I didn't have any questions for *her*, but I *did* have questions.

One, in particular, still nags me to this day.

What the fuck was it all for?

THIRTY-FOUR
VINDICATED

SITTING in the waiting room of the oncology department at USC Norris, waiting to get the results of yesterday's PET scan, I'm reminded of what I'd hated most about having cancer.

It hadn't been the surgery. It hadn't been the radiation. It hadn't even been the gnawing feeling my days were limited. It had been, in fact, *the others*. Having a terminal disease is one thing, but seeing it manifested in other people is something else entirely. You see these scrawny husks of papery skin, with their bald scalps and their washed-out eyes and their ridiculous fucking antiviral masks, and you want to look down on them. Call it scorn, call it pity, call it disgust. Call it whatever the fuck you'd like. You want to feel different from what they are. You want to *be* different. You want to elevate yourself above them, but you can't, because you're one of them.

I can't be one of them again. Not ever again. Once was enough.

Once was too much.

A woman sitting across from me is crying, which accentuates the thrumming remnants of the headache currently serving as an embittered reminder of the weeks of abuse I've put my body through. The woman is young, probably no older than I was when I'd been diagnosed. She hasn't shaven her head, and the thin remnants of her hair are falling out in patchy clumps. A stiff breeze likely would have torn her violently in half. The tears on her hollowed face shine like tiny silver buttons.

I watch her, and I want to feel something. I want to feel anything at all, but there is nothing.

I stand and get a handful of tissues from one of the receptionists. When I give them to the woman, she takes them and looks up at me with something that at first looks like terror, but after a few moments her lips part into a jagged smile. Her teeth are shot through with black rot. "Thank you," she whispers.

I don't answer. I sit back down.

I take out my phone and start to text Judy, but I can't think of anything to say. I put the phone back in my pocket.

A door opens, and a nurse comes out. She looks at her clipboard. "Seward?" she calls.

I get to my feet.

"Good luck," says the crying woman. She gives me another corpse-smile.

I don't say anything.

There is nothing to say.

• • •

After the appointment, I drive in a sort of daze to Echo Park. I'm miraculously able to find decent parking, but I'm too out of it to fully appreciate the sheer gravity of such an occurrence.

I walk through the strewn-about trash and over to an unoccupied bench, brushing empty cups and sandwich wrappers and other scraps of garbage from its surface before sitting down. I look out at the laughing, smiling people—mostly couples, as is to be expected—floating around the small brown lake in their ridiculous, swan-shaped pedal boats. The water is filthy, littered with all various kinds of refuse, and the water shooting from the big fountain is a sickly green color. No one seems to care. I remember coming here when I was ten—it must have been before my week with Frisk, because everything after that is blank—when the water had been clean and there wasn't any litter. Carlotta had taken me on one of the boats, and I'd been awestruck by the view of the massive metropolis rising from the south. I remember thinking, *I will move here someday, and I will be happy.*

I am here, but I am not happy.

Nor, surprisingly, am I as *un*happy as I have been the last few years. As I look at the idiot couples floating on their stupid boats while the vagrants shamble around me, I feel numb, disconnected. My quest for fame and fortune has reached its conclusion, albeit far shy of where I'd expected it to end, and I can't even be bothered to be upset about it. I should feel *something*, at least—sadness, anger, self-pity, *anything*—but there isn't anything whatsoever for me to feel.

The yellow woman appears and sits beside me, leaning close and licking my face with her sandpapery tongue. I sigh and light a cigarette, watching a homeless man push a vacuum cleaner back and forth over a patch of dead grass, mumbling incoherently to himself. My phone vibrates, and when I check it, there's a text from Arthur: *we need to talk*. He's been silent for the last week or so, and I can't imagine anything he wants to talk about is something *I'd* want to talk about. I can't even bring myself to want to kill him anymore. That kind of animosity requires more energy than I'm either capable of at this time, or willing to expend.

I realize, with a bored kind of disinterest, that maybe this is what enlightenment feels like. It's not even that I'm apathetic—I've been apathetic before, and it didn't feel like this—I've *transcended* apathy. The triviality of everything is so apparent to me, so clear, I'm astounded I never fully realized it before.

The yellow woman begins stroking my hair.

I put my cigarette out on her bare, prune-skinned thigh, wondering what she'll do.

All she does is grin.

THIRTY—FIVE

THE EYELESS FISH
AT THE BOTTOM OF THE SEA

JUDY meets me later that night at El Cid. We sit in a dark booth in the corner, watching the band (advertised on the poster out front—unironically, I'm pretty sure—as "the greatest Hole cover band in Los Angeles") set up their equipment on the stage. We go a long time without saying much, sipping our whiskey sours—I'm not jazzed about the 160 calories, but it's a special occasion—and deliberately not looking at each other. I'd given her the news on the phone so I wouldn't have to watch her cry.

"It's funny," I finally say after the waiter brings us our second round of drinks. "I had thought I would be angry, but I'm not. Really, I guess I'm sort of relieved. I'd always wondered when. Not *if*, just *when*. Now I know. I mean, yeah, there are things I wanted to do. To accomplish.

But it wasn't happening for me, anyway. I can see that now. It was never going to happen for me, and it's a relief to stop fighting it."

She takes a tentative sip of her drink. She looks so beautiful. She always looks especially beautiful in the dark. Her features seem to take on an ethereal ghostliness, only teasingly suggestive of the dazzling splendor that's revealed in the light. "You sound awfully fatalistic," she says. "You beat it once. You can beat it again."

I shake my head. "Not this time, Judes. Not this time."

"What are you talking about? You can't just *give up*."

"I absolutely can. I already have. The oncologist laid it out very explicitly. I can do a radical surgery, followed by radiation, then fucking *chemo*, or I can wait for it to kill me. The latter is much more appealing."

"You're not making any sense. You've done surgery before. You've done radiation, you've—"

"Not *this* kind of surgery. They'd basically have to take out everything on the right side of my neck, including the facial nerve. That would be followed by major facial reconstructive surgery, to 'make it look passable.' According to the doctor, as long as I don't show any expression, people might not notice 'if they don't look too closely.'"

"You don't show much expression anyway." Her ensuing laugh is hollow and humorless.

"I'm not doing it, Judy. And the chemo? I've always said I'd never do that shit. No way am I going to lose all my hair, even for just a few months. If my choices are life or vanity, I choose vanity."

She sighs and looks away. I can't tell if she has tears in her eyes, and

I'm glad for this small mercy afforded by the darkness. "Yes," she says. "I wouldn't really expect anything different from you."

"You always said I was a narcissist."

She looks at me and nods. "I did. But I guess I've been clinging to some weird hope you'd prove me wrong someday."

I raise my glass to her. "This is not that day."

"Ty," she says, taking my hand in both of hers. There *are* tears in her eyes. I can't see them, but I know they're there. "Please. You have to do *something*. I don't know, get a second opinion, get a third and a fourth and a fifth or however the hell many it takes. You can't just roll over and die."

"I'm sorry, Judy. I'm not going to spend my last year on earth in and out of doctors' offices. They're not going to tell me anything different anyway."

She swallows. "A year? Is that . . ."

"Yes. Give or take. It's spread to—I don't even know, half a dozen other places in my body. It's moving very fast."

She takes her hands away and folds them on her lap, straightening her posture. She looks down at the table. "I need you to do something for me, then."

"If I can."

"No. You have to do this. You have to."

"Have to do *what*, Judy?"

She stares at her hands and picks at her thumbnail. "You have to leave me alone."

I hadn't expected that. "Leave you . . . alone? As in . . ."

"Yes. You can't contact me anymore."

I snort. "I've heard that before."

"Tyler. I mean it this time. I can't–" Her voice hitches. She takes the napkin from beneath her glass and uses it to dab her eyes. "I can't watch you die. I can't. If you won't do what it takes to beat this, I can't see you anymore. I can't see you ever again." She pauses. "Look, maybe life doesn't mean much to you, but I know *I* mean something to you. So, tell me. How much am I really worth? Do I mean more to you than your precious face?"

Taking a deep breath, I hold my glass up so it catches the light from the stage. I look at my distorted reflection on its curved surface. I set it back down.

Judy takes my hand again. She squeezes it. "Please," she says again. "*Prove me wrong.*"

I pull my hand away. "Judy," I say, consciously softening my voice. "You were never wrong. Not about me."

She puts her face in her hands and begins to sob.

We sit there for a while, as the band kicks off their set with "Doll Parts" and follows it with "Jennifer's Body." When Judy finally stands to leave, they're playing "Reasons to Be Beautiful." I had thought she would offer some last parting words, or at least kiss me goodbye, but she doesn't. She gets up and walks out, and she is gone.

I sit there listening to the band for a while, and then I notice the guy with the blond crewcut watching me from a booth on the other side of the room. I give him a little salute before ordering another drink.

• • •

I've switched to scotch on the rocks by the time the blonde woman sits down across from me in the booth. It takes me a moment to recognize her—partially because I'm a little drunk, and partially because it's dark, but mostly because she's one of the last people I'd expect to run into.

"Mrs. Rider?" I say, squinting, leaning forward.

"Oh, Ty, *please*, I told you not to *call* me that." She smiles, lifts her shoulders slightly, and sips her gimlet. "It's Fran. Please."

"What are you . . . doing here?"

Raising her glass in tandem with her eyebrows, rattling the ice inside, she says, "Drinking, obviously. This is one of my favorite places to do so. It's far enough from home that I can feel anonymous, but not *so* far as to make the Uber ride unbearable." She examines my face, smiling deviously. "What are *you* doing here?"

I look at my drink and murmur, "Celebrating, I guess."

"Ooh, what are we celebrating?"

"*We* aren't celebrating anything," I say. "And, besides, it's . . . nothing good."

"Why would you celebrate something that isn't good?"

I shrug. "I guess I'm just kind of a weird guy."

Francesca nods slowly, and then looks over at the stage, where the band is packing up their gear. A twenty-something girl disengages from her friends and goes over to the jukebox, where she starts flipping through the song choices. "I hope she chooses something listenable," Francesca says. "That band was just *awful*."

"I thought they were pretty good," I say, not looking at her. "My ex was really into Hole."

"Hole? Is that who was playing?"

I look at her, a little too drunk to decide if I'm amused or annoyed. "No," I say. "That was a cover band. A Hole cover band."

Even in the dim light, I can see her cheeks flush. I decide I'm not annoyed. I also decide she's actually quite attractive. "Oh," she says, "you'll have to excuse me, I'm not terribly well-versed in those punky metal bands, or whatever it is they fashion themselves as. I'm afraid I don't care much for it, to be completely honest."

"No?" I sip my drink, feeling spontaneous, even a little flirtatious. "What do you like, then?"

Francesca hesitates before answering, and I can tell the question takes her by surprise. I wonder how long it's been since someone asked her that. "Well, I . . . ah, I quite enjoy classical music," she says. "You know, symphonies and such. But I don't listen to it as much as I'd like. Beatrice *hates* it, and my husband, he calls it 'snooze blues,' which really doesn't even make any *sense*, when you think about it. Anyhow, he always makes me turn it off. He says 'pretension never looked good on me,' or something to that effect."

"Your husband sounds like a jackass."

She laughs, and it's different from the other times I've heard her laugh—more natural, less careful and rehearsed. "He *is* that, yes. Lord, you have *no* idea."

"You should let yourself enjoy the things that give you pleasure," I say, getting into this. I'm enjoying the effect I'm having on her. It's almost enough to raise a flicker of feeling within me—a perverse, hedonistic thrill. I'm certain she can see me for what I am, much like her daughter could, and yet she seems to be drawn to me anyway. Much like her daughter was. And she looks so *much* like her daughter. "Your life belongs to you," I continue, recognizing I sound pretty inebriated but not caring. "You only have so much time on earth, so why spend it trying to please other people? Generosity, selflessness, what does that get you? Some nice words at a funeral pulpit? A cutesy epitaph on your gravestone?" I shake my head. "Sorry, I'd rather have a good time when I'm still here. People will say all kinds of things about me when I'm gone. They'll say I was selfish, they'll say I was immoral, they'll say I was vain. But you know what they won't say? They won't say I ever put someone else's enjoyment before my own. Most call it self-indulgence, I call it an advanced state of being."

"That's . . . an interesting way of looking at things."

"Listen, when I was in high school, I learned about this . . . eyeless fish. I don't remember what it was called, but at some point in history, this fish started migrating to deeper and deeper waters. It ended up in a place so deep and so dark its vision was rendered useless, and it adapted to live without the use of sight. Eventually, a generation of those fish was born without eyes, and so were all the generations after it. What I'm talking about, it's no different. We live in a society that no longer has any use for selflessness, so adaptive genetics has . . . bred it out of me. I am the next phase in human evolution. I am the eyeless fish at the bottom of the sea." I smirk and knock back the rest of my drink. "Or," I say with a shrug, "maybe I'm just an asshole."

"I don't think you're an asshole," she says, and the look on her face tells me she's aware of how obsequious she sounds, but she's powerless to stop it.

Speaking of fish, this is like shooting them in a barrel.

"You don't know me. The last woman who sat across from me said I was a narcissist, and she *did* know me."

"My husband is a narcissist, I think. Or, maybe *he's* just an asshole. I don't really know. And you're right, I don't know you, but I *do* know you don't seem anything like my husband."

The girl at the jukebox selects a song, and the Eagles' "One of These Nights" slides from the speakers. I grin and stand up, holding out my hand. "It's not Mozart," I say. "But it's pretty damn close."

Francesca looks at my hand. "Mr. Sewar—Ty, I . . . It's been so long since I've been on a dance floor. I'm afraid I'd make a fool of the both of us."

"I'm not worried about what anyone thinks. You shouldn't be, either."

"No one *else* is dancing."

"No, and that is a terrible crime. It's our civic duty to correct it."

She bites her lip, but it does nothing to stop her mouth from twitching into an uneasy smile.

"You've already made up your mind," I press. "You're practically dancing already."

THIRTY-SIX

MOTHER KNOWS BEST

FRANCESCA'S head is bobbing up and down in my lap when Beatrice walks into the bedroom.

"Mom?" Beatrice says, rubbing her eyes. She squints. "*Ty?*" Her hair is mussed from sleep, and she's wearing an oversized T-shirt–probably her father's–that falls midway down her thighs. She isn't wearing a bra.

Francesca lifts her head and turns around, shrinking against me and covering her breasts with her arms. "Beatrice, baby–Honey, this . . . this isn't what it looks like."

"Actually," I say, lighting a cigarette, feeling calmer than I probably should, "it's pretty much exactly what it looks like."

"You can't tell your father," says Francesca.

"You should join us," I say to Beatrice. I'm not sure why, but I also add, "You give better head than she does. Maybe you can show her how it's done."

"*Ty*," says Francesca, but I can't tell if she's offended because I've invited her daughter into bed with us, or because I've insulted her blow-job skills. Probably the latter.

"How long have you been fucking her?" Beatrice asks me. There's a quavering fragility to her voice, like she's hurt, but she doesn't have any right to be hurt. She's the one who fucked my uncle behind my back.

"This is the first time," I tell her plainly. "Well, it was going to be the first time. We're just getting started, and you're more than welcome to join in. I know your mother would like that."

"*Mr. Seward*," gasps Francesca, but the look in her eyes doesn't match the tone of her voice. I shrug at her.

"Did you know that I've been sleeping with him?" Beatrice asks her mother, and I realize, yes, there's definitely pain in her voice. As much as she doesn't have any right to her pain, it gives me a degree of faint satisfaction, nevertheless.

"I . . . I had assumed the two of you had been . . . intimate," says Francesca carefully. "I had my suspicions, yes."

Beatrice nods slowly, her mouth tightening, as if her mother's admission has confirmed something for her. She looks at me again, and for a second, I'm transported back to that night on her living room couch, when she'd held me while I'd cried. When she had given me safe harbor from my own inner demons. When she had been everything I'd ever wanted.

Now, she's just a teenage girl whose mother I'm about to fuck.

It's better this way.

"Look," I say, crushing my cigarette out in a heart-shaped ashtray on the nightstand. "I don't mean to spoil this touching mother-daughter moment, but I'm starting to lose my hardon. Beatrice—*Dolly*—you can either join us, or leave."

Saying that, I'd expected her to leave. I had thought the outlandishness of my proposal would make her turn around and go back to her room. The last thing I expect her to do is heave a capitulatory sigh and walk across the bedroom to climb into the bed with us, but that's exactly what she does.

Francesca looks from me to her daughter and back at me. I give her a look that's supposed to say, *Well, here we are*, holding my palms out. After a prolonged moment of hesitation, Francesca lets her arms fall away from her breasts. Beatrice is on her knees, facing the two of us. Francesca moves away from me, crawling toward her daughter and kneeling before her.

I sit up and begin to stroke myself. "Be a good girl," I say to Beatrice, "and kiss your mother."

Francesca puts a hand on Beatrice's shoulder, caressing it. Beatrice gives me one of her indecipherable looks before shutting her eyes and taking a deep breath. She leans forward, just so, and Francesca makes up the remainder of the distance, pushing herself against her daughter and kissing her, slipping her tongue into her mouth and burying her hands in her hair.

Arthur would be so proud of me.

With hungry, jerky movements, Francesca pulls Beatrice's shirt off and throws it onto the floor, exposing her naked torso and a pair of panties with unicorns on them. Francesca kisses the hollow of her daughter's neck and traces her tongue down to her right breast. She runs its tip around the circumference of the nipple before taking it into her mouth and, in a perverse display of role-reversal, suckling it. Beatrice moans, her face contorted in a bizarre combination of shame and ecstasy. She moves her hands up her mother's bare back and into her hair, clenching handfuls of it in her fists and moaning louder.

I've never been harder in my life.

Francesca pushes Beatrice onto her back and pulls her underwear off. She gazes at her daughter's vagina before looking at me, awaiting further instruction.

"Eat her," I say breathlessly. "Eat your daughter's pussy."

The alacrity with which Francesca responds to this command is almost terrifying. She lowers herself onto her stomach and shoves her face between her daughter's legs, placing her parted lips over Beatrice's vagina, nuzzling it, sucking loudly on it in between the rapid in-and-out movements of her tongue.

Unable to take it anymore, I position myself behind Francesca, spitting on my palm and massaging the saliva over my erect cock before poking it at her anus. It yields beautifully, making me wonder how often she engages in this particular activity with her husband. With my eyes staring into Beatrice's, I begin thrusting violently into her mother's asshole. Their bodies jostle and shake as I pump my hips. Francesca, still

216

lapping at her daughter's vagina, slides her hands up Beatrice's stomach and clutches her joggling breasts. Beatrice clenches her mother's face with her thighs and cries out, grabbing fistfuls of the sheets and arching her back. Her face flushes crimson, and she screams she's coming, writhing and twisting and bucking, and I think to myself, *I never made her come like that.* I try not to feel too bad about it, though, because they do say, after all, that Mother knows best.

When I feel like I'm getting too close to climaxing, I pull myself out of Francesca's asshole. Francesca raises her face up from between Beatrice's legs and cranes her neck to look back at me, her cheeks shining and sticky. "Come here," I tell her, pulling on her hips. She gets up and turns to face me, pressing her body against mine and wrapping her arms around my neck.

Francesca's lips taste of her daughter's cunt when she kisses me. Her tongue rubs Beatrice's vaginal juices over the backs of my teeth.

Beatrice joins us, pressing her body into ours, rubbing her hands over us, kissing my neck, her mother's neck. She reaches down and begins stroking my damp, befouled dick, angling it downward and using its tip to stimulate her mother's clitoris. I permit this for a little while, and then I disengage from Francesca and put my hands atop Beatrice's shoulders, pushing her down and guiding my cock into her mouth. Francesca repositions herself and keeps kissing me, placing one of her hands on the back of her daughter's head, forcing her to take me deeper into her throat. Beatrice gags and coughs, but she does not stop.

"I want to watch you fuck her," Francesca whispers into my ear before nibbling on my earlobe, hard enough to be painful. "I want to watch you fuck my daughter."

Beatrice looks up at me, her eyes wide and watering. I nod at her, and she takes my dick out of her mouth with an audible *plop* that might be humorous if the circumstances were a little different. She starts to lie down, spreading her legs, but I tell her, "No. I want you to ride me." I lie on my back, and she positions herself over my cock, lowering herself onto it, gasping when I enter her. She starts slow, with measured rocking-horse movements, steadily increasing her pace. I run my hands up her smooth thighs, over her flat stomach, cupping her breasts, squeezing them. She puts her hands on my wrists, shutting her eyes. Her mother sits, watching and touching herself, her hand fanning a frenetic blur over her vagina. The sheets are soaked beneath her.

"I hate how much I love your dick," Beatrice breathes, putting her palms on my chest as she bounces on top of me. She looks deep into my eyes, but she seems to see something there she doesn't like because she almost immediately looks away. I notice a tear rolling down her cheek as her mother goads her on, gasping, "That's my baby girl, that's it, fuck him just like that."

As much as I resent Beatrice's betrayal, I'm unable to deny how good it feels to be inside her again. "Your cunt was designed for my cock," I tell her, running my hands all over her body, the feel of her taut skin making me even harder, heightening the friction between my aching erection and the warm, wet vise-grip of her vaginal walls.

Francesca comes over and sits on my face, and I can hear sucking sounds as she starts kissing Beatrice. I start tonguing Francesca's cunt as she rocks on her haunches, grinding her groin against my mouth. She tastes older than her daughter, which I guess is to be expected, and the hot, damp scent of musky basement isn't anything like the pleasant aroma I've come to recognize as distinctly Beatrice's.

When I feel the tightening in my groin as my pelvic muscles begin to contract, I shove the girl and the woman off me and rise to my knees, feverishly stroking my cock. "Mouths open," I command. "Tongues out." They obey, crowding in front of my engorged dick, their faces touching. I let out a long, guttural groan as the semen begins to shoot out, pivoting my hips to make sure both of them get a fairly portioned helping. Some of it gets in their mouths, but most of it ends up dotted along their lips, streaked across their foreheads and cheeks and noses, globbed in their eyes and in their hair. When I'm done, I tell them to lick each other clean, and they do, starting with sloppy kisses before running their tongues over each other's face and sucking congealed balls of dead kids out of sweat-dampened locks of hair.

Afterward, lying there smoking a cigarette with one of them on either side of me, my arms around them, I realize this is the pinnacle of my existence, my crowning achievement, and I'm not sure what that says about me. Beatrice is crying softly. Francesca is already asleep. I glance over at the ridiculous heart-shaped ashtray on the nightstand, crowded with clumps of gray ash, and I try to feel something, but I can't.

• • •

Once I'm certain both of them are asleep, I ease myself out from between them and carefully climb out of the bed. I dress in silence, watching them sleep. The thought occurs to me I should take a picture of them and send it to Arthur, just to gloat, but I decide not to because I'm not sure it would even do anything for me.

After exiting the room and tiptoeing along the hall and down the stairs, I'm about to reach for the handle of the front door when I sense a presence behind me. I sigh and turn around, expecting to see the yellow woman, but it's Beatrice. She's pulled the T-shirt back on and is standing at the foot of the stairs, one hand gripping the banister. Her eyes are wet. "It's about time," she whispers.

I blink at her. I'd been so close to escaping. "What's . . . about time?" I ask.

"That you finally stopped pretending."

"Look," I say, rubbing my jaw with my palm. "I don't even know . . . what that means."

"You do, though."

"No, actually. I don't. Listen, I know about you and Arthur. I know what you did." I pause, and I guess it's for effect. "He told me."

She looks startled, confused. "Told you what? That we *fucked?*" Her voice momentarily raises, making her flinch, and she looks over her shoulder and up the stairs. Whispering again, she says, "How is that even, like, a thing? That's what he does. You knew about it. You *watched* it."

"Yeah, but not after you and I—"

"After we *what*, Ty?" She steps down from the bottom stair and advances a few paces closer to me. "After *we* fucked? Suddenly it's not okay because *you're* fucking me, too?"

I look away, my eyes moving to the living room and landing on the couch, where I suppose everything had begun and ended. "I just thought—" I begin, but I'm silenced by the expression on her face when I glance back at her.

"What did you *think*, Ty? Please, tell me what you *thought*." She wipes her eyes with the first three fingers of each hand.

"I don't . . . know. I really don't know what I . . . thought." Feeling cornered, helpless, I add, "That movie, the one Arthur said he was going to put you in—it doesn't exist. There is no movie. He was lying."

She raises her eyes to the ceiling and wipes them again, shaking her head. "I know that," she says. "You can't really think I don't know that."

"Then . . . why would you . . . I just don't know why you—"

"It's not that simple. Not everything is a quick tit for tat. There are, like . . . it's like . . . there are debits and deposits, you know? Sometimes you have to, you know, make a deposit into an account so you can debit from it later."

"That's not how Arthur operates. Everything is on his terms. He's never indebted to anyone."

Beatrice sighs, pushing a lock of hair behind her ear. "Sometimes you have to go through the motions," she says. "Sometimes you have to do what's expected of you. You wouldn't really understand."

"Why?" I scoff. "Because I'm a guy?"

"That's part of it," says Beatrice, nodding in a way that makes her look far older than she is. "But that isn't all of it."

"Enlighten me, then."

"I can't. You wouldn't get it."

"Whatever," I say, shaking my head, disgusted with all this. With her. "I don't have time for this." I turn for the door.

As I'm walking out, she calls, "Ty?" I stop, looking over my shoulder and raising my eyebrows impatiently. "What happened to you? Who *hurt* you?"

I stand there for a moment, staring at her, and then I leave and shut the door behind me.

• • •

As I'm getting into my car, a black Accord drives by with its high-beams on.

THIRTY–SEVEN

RATS IN CAGES

I spend most of the next day lying on my futon, watching *It's Always Sunny in Philadelphia* and crying for some weird reason I can't figure out because I don't feel anything but cold, distant numbness. The scale tells me I'm down another pound, which should at least give me a jolt of fleeting satisfaction, but it only makes me feel empty. I squander about ten minutes stepping on and off it again, staring at the number with blank confusion and wondering why I'm not getting the usual reward, like one of Skinner's rats pressing on a lever that no longer yields the expected food pellet.

I burn through two packs of cigarettes, sometimes smoking them two or three at a time, and drink a lot of water because the thought of alcohol vaguely repulses me. Around noon, I do some of the leftover coke I find in my junk drawer, but the high is so negligible and short-lived it feels like a waste.

By nightfall, I'm out of cigarettes, so I trek out to the gas station next door to buy another couple of packs. I look for the black Accord and don't see it anywhere, but that doesn't mean anything.

Instead of going back to my apartment like I should, I start walking without any clear direction or destination. I wind up on Hollywood Boulevard—a street I avoid more than any other, and that never fails to nauseate me—and find myself drifting among the tourists and the bums, the panhandlers and street musicians and people dressed up like movie characters. I bump into a yellow Transformer who stands two heads taller than I do and walks with mechanized motions down the filthy, puke-scented sidewalk. Some fat guy who's costumed as Captain America or Aquaman or something pursues me for half a block, pleading and pestering for a cigarette while I ignore him. Outside of a strip club advertising "1000s OF BEAUTIFUL GIRLS AND 3 UGLY ONES," a woman in a bedazzled bra and spandex hot pants tries to hand me a coupon, telling me I look like I "could use a good time." I consider asking her if she'd be willing to come back to my apartment and eat some tin foil, but I realize the idea kind of bores me, so I keep walking.

My legs are aching and I'm out of breath by the time I reach Madame Tussauds, so I have a Lyft take me back to my apartment. I'd been half-expecting the guy with the creepy grin to be my driver again, but it's some old Korean woman in a Prius who runs two red lights and narrowly avoids getting us killed by an oncoming bus.

Back at my apartment, I'm feeling jittery and tense for reasons I can't pinpoint, so I make the (always) ill-advised decision to smoke a joint. I think the weed must be laced with something else, though, because it hits me too hard and too fast, and makes the anxious feeling even worse. There's nothing to do but lie on my back and wait for it to pass, or for sleep to come. The yellow woman crouches beside the futon, whispering unknowable things to me.

• • •

I wake up around midnight to four missed calls from Arthur. I'm deleting the voicemails without listening to them when a text message from Arthur comes through. I accidentally click "READ" when I'd been intending to tap on the fourth and final voicemail so I could delete it, and then I sit there staring at the image on my screen for a long time.

I'm still staring at it, trying to decide how it makes me feel, when Arthur sends a follow-up text that says, *call me.*

I go back to staring at the picture, a little stressed out because my body and mind aren't reacting properly to it.

call me or you won't like the next pic I send, says another text.

That *does* make me feel something, but it's only a tired, exasperated sense of annoyance. I don't want to deal with my tyrannical uncle at the moment. I have my own problems. I don't want to deal with him ever again, as a matter of fact, but that's not much more than wishful thinking. When Beatrice had told me I should quit, I had been the one to tell her it's not that simple. Arthur is proving my point for me. Regardless of how I feel, or *don't* feel, he's forced me into a position in which I have to respond.

Gritting my teeth, I select his contact and lift the phone to my ear. He answers halfway through the first ring, cheerily greeting me by saying, "Well, it's about goddamn *time*."

"I was asleep."

"For three weeks?"

I clear my throat. "Something like that."

Undeterred, Arthur says, "So, did you like my pic?"

"What are you even doing, Arthur."

"A number of things, actually. Getting your attention, for one. It's been quite difficult ever since you went off the deep end and beat the ever-loving shit out of that poor girl. And two, I'm shooting a little indie movie, just like I promised."

"I . . . regret having to hurt Allison. But what happened to her was your fault."

"Please, Ty, *spare* me all that bullshit. Take some responsi*bili*ty for your *act*ions, yeah? There were all kinds of ways you could have handled that situation, but you went with the *worst* possible one. You have no grasp on the meaning of *con*sequence. You don't know how to be forward-thinking. That's why—among other things—you'll never make it in this town."

This should piss me off, and I can feel a distant part of me bolstering itself for some sort of negative emotional response, but it's purely because it's been conditioned to do so. It quickly becomes aware I'm not going to react, neither inwardly nor outwardly, so it resumes its slumber. I remain silent.

"Anyway," says Arthur, "I really need your help with this one. You see, I can't make this movie without you. Dolly might be my leading lady, but *you're* the *real* star."

"I'm not playing this game, Arthur. No more games. I'm done."

"You're *not* done," Arthur says, his voice becoming harsh and strained with anger. "*I* tell you when you're done, yeah? And you're not even *close* to being done. Because this movie is getting made *with* or *without* you, and if I have to make it *without* you, things are going to be that much worse for Dolly." He pauses, and I can picture his sinister grin. "You don't want that, Ty. We *both* know how much you don't want that."

Do we, though? I wonder to myself. *Do we* really *know that?* I pull the phone away from my ear and look at the picture again, but it still fails to elicit any sort of emotional response. My indifference, I realize, is the only leg up I have on Arthur right now. He doesn't know how much he's overestimated my investment in how this is going to play out. It grants me a power to which I'm unaccustomed, and with such power comes a faint flicker of satisfaction. I *am* going to free myself from Arthur's grasp—the Dying Alone in the Sun Plan necessitates it, and by the time he tracks me down, I intend to already be dead—so I might as well follow this final ploy to its conclusion. If I play my cards right—and, from where I'm sitting, it appears I've got some pretty decent cards—I can emerge victorious over him for the first time in my life. For once, *I'll* be the one with all the power.

"Tell me what you want me to do," I say, doing my best to sound embittered and begrudging.

It's weird that you hate actors so much, because you're the best one I've ever seen.

Let's hope Beatrice was right.

"Come to the compound," says Arthur, sounding pleased with himself. He thinks he's gotten his way. He thinks he's still in control. "Meet me in the sound stage. We'll be waiting, so don't dilly dally, yeah?" He hangs up.

Before I leave, I haphazardly pack some essentials into a duffel bag.

Walking out of my apartment for the last time, there is no sadness. I'd thought there would be elation, or relief, but there isn't anything like that, either.

There isn't anything at all.

THIRTY—EIGHT

A, B, OR C

*C*AN *I do it?*

That thought is nagging me on my ascent into the hills. My perspiring palms keep slipping on the steering wheel, and I'm trying to steel myself by periodically glancing in my rearview mirror at the duffel bag in the back seat. It had seemed simple back in my apartment, but as my elevation increases with the property value of the homes I pass, my resolve is shakier. By the time I start navigating the treacherous twists and turns of Mulholland, the gravity of the situation looms above me like an anxious storm cloud. There are so many potential outcomes to consider.

You're going to have to make a decision, and it's of vital importance to me that you make the right *decision.*

My sudden remembrance of the Lyft driver—or parking cop, or whatever the fuck he is—comes with an accompanying jolt almost like physical pain. It's been a while since I've given him any thought, and while his little prophecy had been generic enough—people make choices every day, after all—it feels much more fortuitous now, given the circumstances. Still, I already *know* what I'm going to do. It's a matter of whether or not I have the nerve to go through with it. As for the options—*A*, *B*, or *C*, as the guy had referred to them—I'm no closer to knowing what those might be, if anything, than I had been that night when he'd picked me up from Allison's street.

Both B *and* C *are perfectly acceptable. Option* A, *on the other hand . . . well, let's just say that would be a* colossal *clusterfuck for all parties involved.*

I have no idea what option *A* is, but all I can do is hope it doesn't align with what I'm intending to do. I don't know if I buy into the grinning man's mysticism, but I don't want to find out the hard way that I should have.

Whatever, it doesn't matter. I know what I'm going to do, and if I end up damned by my actions, so be it.

• • •

The valet, whose name might be, I think, Raoul, opens my door and says, "Your uncle is waiting in the sound stage, Mr. Seward." His brow is creased, and his mouth is a hard, solemn line. I wonder how much he knows.

"Don't park it in the underground garage," I tell him as I get out.

"Keep it up here. Have it ready for me. I won't be long."

"Yes, sir, Mr. Seward." He gives me a worried glance as he gets behind the wheel.

I jog across the property to the sound stage. The door is unlocked, as expected. I'm telling myself to be calm, to appear cool, the ball is in my court, because it *is* in my court. It is.

That's what I'm telling myself as I walk inside.

The first thing I see is Beatrice. She's naked, tied to a chair, her mouth gagged and her eyes bound shut with a scarlet blindfold. A circle of hot white lights beat down on her. Her skin is glazed with a sheen of sweat. A camera on a tripod about five paces away from the chair points in her direction.

I see Arthur next, sitting on the floor away from the glare of the lights, doing something on his phone. He smiles and stands when he sees me. He's wearing a white smoking jacket and pajama pants with little sheep on them.

Carlotta is sitting on a couch near Arthur, wearing an evening gown and sipping a martini. Beside her is a white masquerade mask with a long, curved beak. Seeing Carlotta does something to me I hadn't expected, and the thing that gurgles up within me is so formless and vague I can't properly call it an emotion, much less identify what it means. She meets my eye, but something in my expression must tell her something because she quickly looks away.

The last thing I see is the gun. It's a small, pearl-handled revolver resting on a barstool positioned just outside the circle of light, but close enough so the silver metal of its barrel glints from the shadows.

"It's about time you joined us," says Arthur, spreading his arms wide. "I was *almost* beginning to think I was going to have to start without you."

"What is this," I say to him, as if I don't already know.

"*This*," says Arthur, clapping his hands together and rubbing them, "*this* is what happens when you force my hand."

"I don't understand." And I don't, but I do understand it doesn't matter.

"No great surprise there," says Arthur, grinning. "You never were the brightest."

"Arthur, be nice," says Carlotta, and I shoot her a look that—if there were a God—should be hateful enough to send her brains spewing out the back of her head. She catches it, flinches, and averts her eyes again.

"Just calling it like I see it, dearest," says Arthur. "Listen, Ty, this is all *your* doing. You have to know that, yeah?"

"No. I don't know what you're talking about." I'm walking slowly, with my eyes fixed on Arthur as if we're in a standoff, toward the barstool.

"You compromised *everything*," Arthur says, and I can't tell from his tone if he's angry or excited. "You fucked one of my actresses. That's a conflict of interest, remember? And *then* you had to go and fuck her mother, too? I'm drawing conclusions there, of course, just based on the information I have. But I'm not wrong, yeah?"

I consider telling him I fucked one of his actresses and her mother *at the same time*, but that seems pointless, so I shrug and nod. I'm a few paces away from the barstool.

"You just can't *do* things like that," Arthur says. He sighs, shakes his head. "Look, Ty, I'll level with you. If you'd only fucked her once or twice, I could let it slide. I'm a reasonable man. You know that. But the thing is, you had to go and catch feelings. You had to get *attached*. This is *Hollywood*, Ty. If you let feelings pervade your relationships, you're done for. How do you think Lottie and I have stayed together so long?"

Carlotta, looking at the mask beside her, nods and sips her martini.

"So, consider this another one of your lessons, yeah? No feelings allowed. Not in relationships, and *especially* not in relationships with my actresses." Stroking his chin, he says, "It *does* puzzle me that you went and banged her mom, though. *That* part I can't figure out. I mean, if you're hung up on Dolly, why fuck her mom? You know what, don't tell me, I don't want to know."

"Okay," I say simply. "I won't tell you."

Arthur eyes me for a second, and then he nods, apparently satisfied. "Yes, good. Some mysteries are better left uncovered. Now, let's get to the good part—you see that gun in front of you? You know what I want you to do with it, yeah?"

I look at the gun, and then over at the camera.

"Don't worry about that," says Arthur waving his hand. "You're my nephew, for God's sake. I wouldn't *incriminate* you. This isn't *black-mail*. Lottie, bring me that mask, yeah?"

Carlotta drains the rest of her glass and sets it on the floor before picking up the mask and carrying it over to Arthur. Arthur takes it and brings it to me, holding it out. "Put this on," he says. "Conceal your secret identity, and all that." I take the mask from him, staring into its hollowed-out eyes. Arthur walks over to the camera and stands behind it, tapping some buttons on its side. "Now," he says, "when I say 'action,' I want you to—"

"You can't do this," I say, even though he, of course, absolutely can. I'm biding my time at this point. "I don't know how you got her here, but her parents are going to be looking for her. She's been seen with me. She's been seen with *you.*"

Arthur gives me an *oh, spare me* look. "Really, Ty?" he says, as if addressing a toddler. "You *really* think I haven't taken all of that into consideration? Do you *seriously* believe I would be doing *any* of this if that wasn't all taken care of?"

Beatrice emits a noise, and I look over at her. Her shoulders are hitching, and tears are streaming from beneath the blindfold. Her sobs make her gag on the mouth restraint.

I look back at Arthur and say with a sigh, "Well, if it's all taken care of . . ." I put the mask over my face and tie the thick strings into a knot behind my head. When I pick up the gun, I once more look over at Arthur. There's a look of mild disbelief on his face. I'd been right; he hadn't anticipated this. He'd been expecting me to cry, to plead, to try and bargain for Beatrice's life. He'd expected a fight, but I don't have any fight left in me, and I came here to do something.

You're going to have to make a decision, and it's of vital importance to me that you make the right *decision.*

Here's hoping.

I step into the light, directly in the camera's path.

I raise the gun, thumbing back the hammer, and I point it at the person who needs the bullet the most.

I pull the trigger.

DYING ALONE IN THE SUN

THE sun is high and hot, beaming upon me like a benevolent God that never was. A low, salt-scented breeze sweeps over the quiet, mostly empty beach, rustling my hair. The ocean whispers to me as it laps at the sand, and while it is an ominous whisper, full of long-drowned secrets, I am unperturbed by its voice. It is a mostly welcome substitute for the yellow woman, whom I haven't seen since I left Los Angeles and absconded to this little island to die.

I sip my pina colada, relishing its sweetness, savoring it—at 245 calories, I permit myself two per day, and nothing else. These may be my last days, but I'll be damned if I'm going to leave behind a bloated, sugar-fattened corpse.

As I gaze out at the gently rolling ocean, off in the general direction of where I assume LA must be, thousands of miles away, I'm struck by how pointless my years there had been. All that time chasing fame, chasing money, only for me to leave a murderer, a pariah, a cancer-stricken wretch limping off to make his death nest. I've been here just over a month, and the serenity I've found in this tropical solace makes me wonder why I waited for the cancer to come back before coming here. So much suffering could have been avoided if I'd cashed in earlier. By my calculations, my money should last me another two months, but there had been a point a couple of years ago when my savings would have allowed for at least seven or eight months of carefree living in paradise. That's what I should have done.

What is it they say about hindsight?

It's a bitch, and then you die.

Or . . . something like that.

I glance at my watch, which I've taken off and set beside me on the beach towel, so as to prevent tan lines. I look in the direction of the resort, trying to figure out which window belongs to our room, but it's too far away and the glare of the sun is too bright. It doesn't matter; it's about time I head back there, anyway.

I like to be there when she wakes up.

Acknowledgments

For their contributions to the development and publication of this book, the author wishes to thank the following individuals: Andersen Prunty, CV Hunt, Ryan Harding, Sarah Ruth, James Lee, and Scott Schurdell.

CHANDLER MORRISON is the author of *Dead Inside*, *Until the Sun*, *Hate to Feel*, and *Just to See Hell*. He lives in Los Angeles.

Made in the USA
Columbia, SC
23 June 2022